DR. TYTIANNA
RINGSTAFF

Choice is our most powerful possession.

ENTITY

a horror novella

Honey Tree Publishing
www.honeytreepublishingus.com

Library of Congress Cataloging-in-Publication Data

Ringstaff, Tytianna, Dr. 1987- Entity: A Horror Novella

1. Horror. 2. Fiction. 3. African American. 4. Spirituality. 5. Trade.

Printed in the United States of America

DEDICATION

This book is dedicated to my dear husband and the love of my life, Christopher Neal Ringstaff. Thank you for loving me unconditionally and showering me with experiences that inspire me to do what I enjoy most. I love you.

ACKNOWLEDGEMENTS

It took seven days to write this fictional book from August 5-12, 2025, conceived after returning from vacationing on the beautiful islands of Martha's Vineyard and Nantucket in July 2025.

While vacationing, I immersed myself in one of my favorite pastimes: reading. I didn't expect to read and finish a book of romantic fiction and start a second— a scary book gifted to me, but I did, and it was refreshing.

Writing a book was the last thing on my mind while vacationing— so I thought. However, when I returned to Kentucky, the words began to flow after an essential five-year hiatus from writing and publishing my own work.

Initially sparked by a love for Black history, Victorian houses, a vacation in Massachusetts, supernatural stories, and an unexpected, distorted audio message from my seven-year-old niece, Aria— this book came to fruition. And, as a follower of Christ, it was clear from the start that my spiritual identity would also be reflected in this book.

Journaling while writing this book was essential. I reflected on my ideas about the storyline, dialogue between the characters, and scene descriptions. As I went for a walk or completed a task, the story's details would emerge, revealing the characters and their lives.

This book taught me that a hiatus— a little fresh air, new scenery, and a carefree environment— is necessary to reignite the creative spark. Being present in the moment and passionately enjoying all life has to offer inspires purpose and art.

So, when the urge to write this book finally arrived, I wrote nonstop for seven days, not expecting to write a horror novella. But here we are. And here is the book. *Many Blessings.*

Likewise reckon ye also yourselves to be dead indeed unto sin, but alive unto God through Jesus Christ our Lord.

Romans 6:11 (KJV)

But seek ye first the kingdom of God, and his righteousness; and all these things shall be added unto you.

Matthew 6:33 (KJV)

The Insurrection of 1847

PROLOGUE

"The Autumn night requires a fire," ordered Monsieur Charles Le Rue de Baptiste to a male slave who responded right away. The burnt embers sparked with a slow, glowing reddish-orange flame, transforming into vermilion against the burning logs in the parlor.

Leaning into the hazelnut-stained leather chair in front of the massive burning fireplace, Master Baptiste stared into the dark brown eyes of the self-portrait hanging above the mantle. It was hand-painted in France by a fine gentleman. He wondered if he should have had the painting removed and rehung in a different room, but quickly thought against it.

It's precisely the type of painting that would hang above an opulent fireplace, indeed, he thought, while sipping aged-oak barrel Kentucky bourbon from a silver julep cup.

Meanwhile, outside the large colonial picture window, Big John sought revenge as he watched Master Baptiste at sundown. Holding the cowhide cartwhip used countless times on him, his wife Anna, and their five children, he tightly double-wrapped one end of the whip around his fist, securing it under his thumb, and held the other end, entering the Big House.

Monsieur Baptiste closed his eyes, sinking into the chair, savoring the sweet vanilla-spice against the smoky-wood flavors of the bourbon. It settled into his bloodstream, relaxing him into a sedative sleep, until his eyes opened widely to the suffocating choke of strangulation. Relinquishing the cup, he spilled the bourbon, staining the Savonnerie rug.

Monsieur Baptiste bucked his body to release himself, but was unsuccessful. Big John, a field hand who split his day between the tobacco fields and the "stud farm," was much stronger, standing at 6 foot 6 and 325 pounds of pure muscle against Master Baptiste's 165-pound frame. Big John pulled the whip tighter, strangling Master Baptiste to unconsciousness before dropping his body facedown into the fireplace to char, burn, and die.

Under the blue-black starlit sky, the soft humming of "Wade in the Water," by the house slaves, was joined by the field slaves in the tall tobacco fields. Making their escape, the women swiftly gathered seeds and herbs into their hair. The men stuffed small, treasured trinkets into their trousers. Humming the final verse, they began a new song, "Follow the Drinking Gourd." All coded messages for a slave revolt.

The full moon shone big and white upon the mansion as the enslaved Africans ran through the tobacco fields to the Ohio River bank behind the house, where the North Star stood beautiful and high, representing freedom.

Clutching a small book to her bosom, Anna ran to the river where her husband guided men, women, and children into the water. But when she looked back at the Big House— the only place she had known—a large shadow blanketed the mansion, diminishing any sign of light. And as she squinted harder, the black silhouette of a bodiless figure appeared at the back door. Frightened, Anna turned back toward her husband.

"We gotta go!" said Big John in a whispered shout. "Come on!" Grabbing his wife's hands, he led her into the water with

their five children hanging from his arms and
on his back, as they escaped to freedom.

Over a Century Later

CHAPTER 1

"Hey, Ms. Janelle! Can you tell us a story— a *scary* story?!" asked a young man, a new resident in the rehabilitation center for people in transition. It was October, so the desire for such a story was significantly higher than usual.

"Yeah, yeah, yeah," responded Ms. Janelle, grinning nonchalantly and wiping her hands on her apron. Untying the back, she placed it on the counter. "But *only* because it's Halloween." Chuckling to herself, she walked into the primary social area, furnished with couches, where residents began to gather.

Janelle, the owner of the center and lead nurse, ensured that the residents had what they needed daily– prescribed medication, a healthy meal, activities, and anything else to make their lives more comfortable. But apparently, today, she was responsible for storytelling, too.

"We know you tell the *best* stories," persuaded a woman in her late 40s, crocheting while smiling into her chin and looking at

Janelle through her needle. "So, go on and lay a good one on us."

"Well, alright," said Ms. Janelle, amicably, accepting the role and flopping down in her usual chair. The residents grabbed a seat, forming a semi-circle as Ms. Janelle began.

"Don't tell *nobody*. You've asked for a scary story, so here it goes… But no matter how the story is told, a dark, sinister spirit lived in 1847."

CHAPTER 2

Evalina stood daydreaming at the house that pulled and tugged at her core— a burning desire in the deepest part of herself— demanding her shoes to follow suit, but she never got too close.

The five-story house, a stately White mansion built with cedar wood shingles, with a front facade lined with colonial windows, each with operable pale grey shutters, was surrounded by a wrap-around porch on the first level and three upper-level wrap-around balconies with sky blue painted ceilings to keep the haints away, overlooking the Ohio River. The house was marked by slavery and unnatural deaths, and, quiet as it was kept, was rumored to be haunted. But exquisite, nonetheless. *Luxurious living from old money,* some would even say—the type of wealth that sold land, crops— even people— at one point in time.

Evalina had heard stories. Stories, giving rise to mentions and happenings that the house grew accustomed to. Sightings that could only be constructed from the lucid imagination of an artist, a crazy person, or both. For this house had all the lure of a grand legend.

And while it sat vacant for years, perhaps decades— it seemed— no one quite knew, the only thing certain was that those who visited the mansion were never the same again.

Lore, legend, looney– whatever you wanna call it– the house knew something that just never made it out. And while some demons are destroyed and buried. Others are resurrected, breathing new life.

Or so it seemed.

CHAPTER 3

The sign sat in front of the mansion:
OPEN HOUSE – Today at 9:00 p.m.

I can't wait to tell them, thought Evalina, referring to her friends— Chelsea, Jamison, and Frederick. Evalina had light tan skin and striking brown eyes. She wore her brown hair down in silky waves that reached the middle of her back, making her appear shorter.

Chelsea, the skeptical one of the bunch with skin the shade of butterscotch, was tall and athletic, wearing her hair in braids. Jamison, who always seemed to have an answer for everything, had espresso-brown skin and a mid taper fade with a baseball player's build. And Frederick— a mischievous hothead with a complexion and hair to match— was red-boned with copper-colored, coily hair. He was the tallest of the four with a muscular build.

"Did y'all see the sign?" asked Evalina with anticipation.

"Yeah," said Chelsea. "But what does that even mean for a house not for sale?"

"I don't know," said Evalina, "but I'm sure we can just look inside, *right?*" She hoped to spark some curiosity in her friends.

"Probably so," said Frederick, indifferent.

Jamison interjected, speaking more eloquently than usual. "According to stories at the dorm, there are no known survivors of people who have gone into that house."

"I'm down!" said Frederick with a sudden change of heart.

"Let's definitely go," grinned Chelsea in agreement.

Evalina smiled nostalgically. Now, she could discover everything she had always wanted to know about the house, finally putting to rest the mysteries that had made the fortress a myth.

CHAPTER 4

"I thought this place was popular?" said Frederick, looking around. They were the only ones in front of the house. "Where's everybody at?"

"I guess it's not *that* popular," Chelsea said sarcastically. Flicking a gnat from her shirt, she scanned the grounds until the front door opened.

"Welcome! Are you here for the house tour?" asked the woman at the door, prim and ready, in full character, speaking with a British accent, starkly contrasting the typical southern drawl in Kentucky.

The friends glanced questionably at one another. Evalina broke the silence.

"Yes, ma'am. We're here for the house tour."

"Sensational!" replied the woman, stepping from the door onto the large porch, fully revealing herself under the soft glow of the flickering gas lanterns. "This evening, you will experience the historic 1847 mansion. Please, do come in."

The tour guide, a middle-aged woman with buttermilk skin and not one stitch of makeup, was plain but pretty. She wore a creme-colored Victorian-style ball gown that would have been perfect for a 19th-century soiree had she attended. It was oddly unusual to wear it on a regular day in Kentucky, though.

Her neck was encased in a high, stiff lace collar with a rare emerald gemstone. Her slim arms were covered by long sleeves that ruffled in lace at the wrists, and her tiny waist was cinched by a bone-in-corset hidden under her dress, along with an accompanying large bustle that curved her backside and a petticoat that puffed and fanned the bottom half of the gown. Her hair, chestnut brown, was pulled back and pinned up into three buns— two French rolls on the sides, and one oval-shaped bun at the crown of her head.

"They're *really* going all out for this," whispered Frederick, leaning over to his friends, staring at the woman.

"Evidently," said Chelsea, eyeballing the woman up and down, uninterested.

But Evalina was loving every bit of it. She smiled watching the woman— the actress—

pull out all the stops to make the place feel like it had in its early years.

"Shh, y'all." Evalina hushed her friends, hoping they'd get with the program as they walked up the wide porch steps. She loved old houses and history, so this was right up her alley.

The tour guide ushered the group through the front door into the cathedral-style foyer, where an extravagant antique brass crystal chandelier suspended from the ceiling above the grand staircase.

"The chandelier is original to the house," said the tour guide. "Actually, all fixtures, woodwork, and furniture are original— electricity was added much later, along with a few other renovations."

The tour guide walked the group through the mansion. Framed paintings and portraits of different people covered the walls, reaching to the high ceilings. Evalina couldn't help but marvel at the artifacts.

"This house was built for Monsieur Charles Le Rue de Baptiste of France and his wife, Lady Marie Baptiste of England— an unlikely pair of their day, but they endured the best they could. Monsieur Baptiste owned 120 slaves and 600 acres of land, operating a plantation large enough for cultivating and exporting tobacco, and breeding and training Thoroughbreds. The Baptistes were the most prestigious family in Kentucky of their time, owning and operating the Sacrée Plantation."

"Oh, yeah!" exclaimed Jamison, interjecting. "I remember hearing about that in one of my college classes."

Frederick furrowed his eyebrows, and Chelsea narrowed her eyes at Jamison.

"What?!— I did!" he said in defense of their doubtful stares. Jamison was known to stretch the truth more than a little.

But as Chelsea glanced at the ceiling, she detected a painted scroll with strange letters and symbols. "What's that?"

"That is quite a painting, isn't it, my dear? It's the Seven Deadly Sins scribed in Latin. Greed, Pride, Envy, Gluttony, Wrath, Lust, and Sloth. According to lore, when a person commits one of the seven sins, an evil spirit is released into the house— but we will get to that shortly," said the tour guide with a hasty smile and U-turn spin, lifting and revealing the ruffled cancan under her dress, ushering the group through the mansion. "Right this way."

CHAPTER 5

"While the house has stood for more than a century, it has largely sat empty besides the handful of occupants it has seen over the years," explained the tour guide. Stepping into the dining room, she silently walked past the long, twelve-chair wooden table set with Chinese porcelain and silver. Standing at one of the large colonial windows overlooking the veranda-style front porch, she stared out into the empty street. The group joined her.

"Before reconstruction, the front porch overlooked acres of land— the scent of tobacco leaves entering the open windows of the house— Ah," the tour guide closed her eyes, inhaling deeply. "Can't you just imagine? What a lovely aroma it must have been— yes?"

Evalina was captivated, sitting in every word the tour guide spoke, until Jamison broke the veil.

"Who are they?" He noticed a small, framed wedding picture of a happily married couple.

"Funny, you should ask," responded the tour guide, turning from Jamison to the photograph. "They lived here some time ago. Around the time, a paved road replaced the acres of land. They were a happy couple, at one time, but you know what they say…"

"What do they say?" asked Frederick.

"Happy wife. Happy life," said the tour guide, shrugging her shoulders with a sing-song ring in her voice. She continued, "But then again, what does it truly mean to be happy? Is it staying with someone out of fear or necessity? Who truly knows?" The tour guide's eyes were steady on something through the window. "Love? What of it is exactly vexing? I have always wondered so myself, as it can surely make one do the craziest of things. But Stephen and Lynette– they knew. Yes, they knew."

CHAPTER 6
1982

"What is this, Lynette?!" Stephen was fed up, rushing out of the bar. He held Lynette around the waist, trying to keep her stable, but her drunken, spindly frame flopped downward, as her high heels bent alternately at the ankles, causing them both to trip over each other to the car.

"Get off me, Stephen!" Lynette yelled, slurring her words. Spit dribbled from her lips. "I'm so sick of you! I'm sick of this!" She screamed, pulling away, stumbling, and falling to the concrete. Her long, straight brown hair clung to her sweaty ivory-toned cheeks and forehead. She continued spewing insults while sneering. "You're such a *loser*, Steve."

Stephen stared blankly at his wife, listening, chewing, and digesting every syllable of her drunken, truthful words. He was a short, round, and unshaven balding man with light-tan skin and scruffy neck hair. Over the years, he became a "just there" and "run of the mill" kind of guy— different from the man Lynette married.

Standing up unbalanced, Lynette fixed her shoe. "If you hadn't been such an *idiot* at work, I wouldn't have to *whore* around!" she shouted. Opening the car door herself, she fell into the passenger seat. Her thin, narrow, elongated face frowned, staring out the side window like an angry teenager, not the grown woman she was.

Lynette was once considered "the girl next door"— sweet and tender. But she didn't age gracefully, as everyone thought she would, including her. Years of stress and unhappiness had taken a toll, robbing her of her looks and best features.

Stephen stoically entered the driver's seat, started the car, and headed to their house— a place they once called home. Silent, they both searched out the windows in opposite directions for anything other than each other.

Honk!

Stephen crossed the double yellow line into oncoming traffic. Swerving back in the right lane, gripping the wheel, he closely hugged the white line on the shoulder.

"Just kill us, why don't you!" Lynette shouted, throwing her hands in the air— her face twisted.

That would be a perfect disaster for an ideal distraction, thought Stephen. Those unwanted intrusive thoughts always showed up at the opportune time.

Stephen saw himself dead at the wheel and imagined his wife limping out of the car with those stupid, tall high heels. Then, he imagined her lifeless. *Even better,* he thought with a smirk of satisfaction. Her head punched through the blood-stained window shield. Those long legs he used to love to run his fingers up and down, up and down, now crushed under some organ of a car, now fully exposed. She'd look ridiculously beautiful all mangled up. His thoughts vanished as fast as they had arrived at the house.

⁓

"What the hell, Lynette?!" Stephen hollered, slamming the front door. He thought his marriage to Lynette was on the rocks before, but after recognizing the flirting with other men, late nights with "friends," and the circled ad in the paper of her new side gig, he had all the answers to the clues he wished he had never discovered. He was being cheated on. Their marriage was over.

Stephen tried working on the marriage. Anger management classes. Dinner dates here and there. Small gifts. Couples therapy. He even read a book, something he had never done, titled *"How to Keep Your Marriage Strong Once and for All."* Even after arriving home from work, dog tired, he was willing to put in the effort to make it work with Lynette.

"It takes two," said the Christian marriage counselor. "Maybe getting back to reading scripture and praying together could help," she recommended. But Stephen and Lynette refused to take her advice time and time again.

Lynette was sick and tired of the man she once loved, who went from "hero to zero" over a span of years. Stephen was once everything she ever wanted in a man. But after seeing him at his worst so many times, she traded the description of Stephen as "attractive" for "disgusting," judging his flaws.

He had changed. But, who was she kidding—so had she. Lynette was nowhere near the woman she once was when they first met, fell in love, and exchanged vows in front of loved ones. Those days were gone, long ago. And now, she was stuck with a "pathetic" excuse for a husband. She couldn't even remember the last time they kissed, held hands, touched, told each other *I love you* — or showed any form of affection for that matter. She had put up with a loveless marriage for far too long and was ready to call it quits.

Lynette yelled, cussing Stephen until he couldn't take it anymore. He didn't want to put his hands on Lynette like the other time, leaving her bruised and battered in a women's shelter and him in handcuffs— regretful. That was years ago, and Lynette had forgiven him since then. But their marriage was never really the same after that.

"Hurt people hurt people," said the marriage counselor, but that advice seemed to instigate the abuse— on both ends.

And though Lynette had grown to love and hate Steve, she always ran back to him, thinking: *It would take too long and too much to start all over again,* when leaving seemed a fathomable option during fits of bravery.

But that night, Stephen's anger rose, pulsating through his veins and boiling inside him. Hurrying to the dimly lit basement, Stephen slammed the door and walked down the worn, crooked steps. One screw-in lightbulb, missing its metal string, was already turned on, lighting his path through the unfinished basement. The same unfinished basement he failed to remodel during the second year of living in the old house, which, as he put it, was a "money pit" from the start.

He wanted to hit something, but had nothing to take his frustrations out on. He definitely couldn't punch through stone. Plus, there were enough drywall holes in random areas of the house due to Stephen's deliberately missed anger management sessions now and again.

"Shit!" Stephen screamed, slumping to the last step on the stairs. Groaning, he smothered his head between his fists, hitting his head from side to side, cursing himself and his estranged wife. As he sulked, a flurry of uncontrollable intrusive thoughts, once again, entered his mind, which he felt the strength to carry out.

The black shadow, hovering over the house, seeped past the front door into the basement like a gas leak, unscrewing the bulb-lit basement. Diminishing any sign of electricity. Stephen released his hands from his face, staring into the darkness, confused.

"Damn lights," he mumbled, walking to the lightbulb, hoping his memory didn't fail him. But just as he reached toward the ceiling, he heard it.

You're right to think that way, Stephen, spoke the ominous voice, multiple voices in one, vibrating through the room. *I know your thoughts— when you get like that.*

Stephen braced himself as his eyes dilated, darting through the pitch black basement. Sprinting through the darkness, he tripped up the steps to the door. Twisting and turning the knob. Beating and pushing against the door with his body. But it didn't open. The door was locked— indefinitely.

"Help! Lynette!" he screamed, pounding his fists on the door. But no one could hear. Stephen blindly searched the walls, flipping the old light switches repeatedly, but they didn't turn on, nor had they ever worked. He never installed the lights like his wife had steadily asked him years ago.

A thick fog glided mystically around Stephen, enveloping him in its arms.

"Nooooo!" Stephen wailed. A rushing cold sensation swept through the basement, surging through him. "Oh my God!" he shrieked. Wintry air made his breathy cries translucent. Twisting the knob, beating on the door, and throwing his body against it, Stephen was alone to no avail.

"Help me! Someone— please! Help me!" Stephen screamed at the top of his lungs. But this time, when he opened his mouth, the figureless spirit entered through the tunneled throat canal of his cries, filling him up.

In another world outside the shell of Stephen's body, Lynette decided to check on her husband. Routinely, whenever he got agitated, he'd go down to the "hellhole" they called a basement.

"*Stephen*, are you still *pissed?*" Lynette yelled down to the basement, rolling her eyes. But her words didn't reach past the door. It also didn't help that she really didn't care how her husband felt. She was just playing along. Acting had become mandatory in their marriage.

With Stephen unresponsive, Lynette easily gave up communicating. Leaning against the counter, she closed her eyes, massaging her face with dirty hands, until the basement door unlocked and opened.

Creeaaaak.

Lynette thought about trying her hand at a threat. She just didn't have the energy tonight. But Stephen did.

"Do you want to end all of this?" asked Stephen.

Lynette lifted her face from her hands, looking at her husband. He stood statuesque, legs far apart and arms bowed, appearing larger.

"I'm going to ask you again, Lynette. Do you want to end all of this?" Stephen's voice was not his own. His eyes were stormy.

"Yeah, *Steve*," said Lynette, stressing her husband's name, antagonizing him. "I *do* want this to end," Lynette was surprised by her own words, feeling vindicated, yet powerless.

"Okay," responded Stephen, calmly walking to the front door, out to the porch, and into the street.

"Go ahead and fucking leave me then!" yelled Stephen, his eyes protruding from his skull as he spun in the middle of the road, arms wide open, laughing dementedly.

Lynette gasped, her hand over her mouth, unsure of what she was seeing. The black shadow slowly walked out of the house behind Stephen toward the road. Lynette dashed past the open front door onto the porch in disbelief.

"Fucking leave me, Lynette!" Stephen screamed, laughing. "Ha! You can't, can you?! Huh, Lynette?! Huh?!"

Honk!

And in less than two seconds on the open dark road, Stephen was smashed by a semi-truck. His body, mutilated. Pieces of him stuck to the street. Separated limbs skipped around like rocks to settle and flatten to the concrete. Screaming, his wife stood frozen in the doorway, watching the dark shadow emerge from Stephen's body and walk back toward the house for her.

Wrath
Proverbs 15:1

A soft answer turneth away wrath: but grievous words stir up anger.

CHAPTER 7

"Some say it was the truck driver's fault— he was under the influence. But others say it was something else. Something more *sinister*," said the tour guide.

Clap. Clap.

"But we must make haste!" The tour guide, rotating from the window, led the group through a vast hallway lined with candle-lit wall sconces until they arrived at a bathroom. "This bathroom is certainly not original to the house. Why, there was solely an outdoor privy and a chamber pot during those years," she smiled. "Nonetheless, this former closet was reconditioned for convenience, accordingly."

Surveying the bathroom, Evalina noticed a photograph of a woman. It was in a bubble glass wooden frame hung near the vanity. The woman's almond-shaped brown eyes and mahogany skin were striking, but something in her face told a story of sadness.

"Who is she?" Evalina asked, her eyes steady on the portrait.

The tour guide moved closer to the frame, squinting and studying the woman curiously. "That, my dear, is Candice," she responded. "She has sad, beautiful eyes, doesn't she?" Not expecting a response, she continued. "Candice has a story much like all of you. It starts here in this house— where she grew up too fast and died too soon... Candice."

CHAPTER 8
1979

"I'm so *sick* of working here!" yelled Candice, locking the door to the private restroom. "Damn— I hope they didn't hear me." She immediately resented going into the stall closest to her cubicle, where anyone with slightly good hearing could hear even the quietest sounds.

Candice hated work. She had zero passion. No drive. No discipline. She was always late or didn't show up. She never completed assignments. She complained and always had a place to hide, especially from her micromanaging supervisor, who constantly gazed blankly at her over his bifocals.

Out of sight, out of mind, Candice thought, sliding under the radar in her favorite hiding place. "This shit's for the birds," she mumbled, flipping the toilet lid and sitting down. Removing a Walkman from her coat pocket, she placed the black headphone sponge cushions over her ears, turned over the cassette tape, and pressed play. Allowing the music to serenade her. Away from the noise. Away from the work. Away from all the "boring shit." Candice pulled a small plastic-wrapped bag of colorful pills from her other pocket, grinning—naturally stimulated. "Well, hello to you, too," she spoke to the baggie. She popped the pills into her mouth and placed her lips under the running sink water, flushing it all down.

"Come *on* and take the *edge* off," she whispered, closing her eyes, allowing the medicine to hit her system. It did. It always did, which was the only certainty in her day. She could count on the high it granted her. Doing exactly what she knew it could and would do. Each time. Each day. It was a quick pick-me-up whenever she needed, but soon, she would be back doing the next boring thing. The same dumb shit over and over again, day after day, hour after hour.

Mellowing out, Candice watched the memory-recorded footage behind her eyes as her mother panned the screen. Candice was raised by a woman who tried to keep her out of harm's way but failed miserably. Not because she wanted to, but because she just "didn't have time to be dealing with this."

"I can't always protect you!" were the words Candice remembered her mother screaming at her when things got really bad. Like the other women in the streets, her mother had given up her rights to motherhood, security, and protection. Her words lay painful behind Candice's tired, tear-puddled eyes, streaking her cheeks. Candice dug deeper into the pits of her past and crevices of her cerebrum.

"I hear you'll do *anything* to get a fix," spoke the man who became a regular of Mama's. "Bring that little girl in here…"

The man's voice entered the bedroom of five-year-old Candice. Then, her mother's voice. No longer the sweetness of newly spun cotton candy, it was now spotted like black mold and mildew, souring and infecting all it was exposed to. She spoke unlike herself. Her voice, raspy and throaty from a hard life as a prostitute and fend, invigorated her to mindlessly trade in her virtue for skin craters and beauty for dead teeth. She was

Candice wandered and wavered in and out of consciousness, still holding on to the twenty-three years of guilt that lay thick on her like the heaviness of alcohol mixed with sweat, semen, blood, and torn flesh once born innocently.

The medicine prescribed for someone else was working now, filling Candice like gasoline in a tank. The overflow she craved. Floating with a childlike smile and dried tears on her face from all the wounds— all the shit she had been through. Her brain wires– misfiring– in her prefrontal cortex, signaling a physical reaction. Numb. Numbing. Frigid air prickled her skin to goose pimples. Thin metal strings racing down her arms and legs, cooling her flushed neck and face. Eyes half closed. She was somewhere other than here. She was no longer here. She was gone. Flying in the ocean. Swimming in the sky. Floating. "Float, float, float on," like mama used to sing. Swinging her body against a tangerine sun-drenched window in our little apartment, the sunrays swallowing her skinny frame into lines. Back when mama used to twirl me around and teach me how to pray. When she was my only light.

Light. Sirens.

"She's back!" yelled an EMT.

The medication that reversed the high worked. It always did. That was another certainty about life— no one likes it when adults have fun.

"What the hell's going on?!" Candice yelled at the two EMTs, trying to climb off the stretcher.

"Ma'am, you're safe now. We have you. You survived," responded the male EMT, who looked happy-go-lucky. *This must have been his first save*, thought Candice flatly.

"You are alive. You made it! We almost thought we lost you," said the other EMT. She had a natural smile on her face, too. *They must be new to all this*, thought Candice, unmoved.

"Why did y'all do that?!" Candice was livid, moving her spaghetti string-looking legs and arms, still trying to get off the stretcher.

"Ma'am, you OD'd," responded the female EMT.

"And I was fine— until now!" Then, Candice's thoughts frantically pivoted to her job. "I'm supposed to be at work!"

The EMTs looked bewildered at each other, but Candice hadn't gotten the picture.

"I'm going to lose my job if I don't get back! My shift is almost up!" Candice yelled, unaware of the time lapse she experienced or the reality of her situation.

"Ma'am, I hate to tell you this, but you OD'd at work, and according to the words we overheard your supervisor say, you were fired."

"Fired?" A foreign voice escaped from Candice's lips.

"It was time to close for the day, and you hadn't clocked out. So, when they checked the security cameras, they saw you enter a restroom. But when they knocked on the door and you didn't answer, they kicked the door in and found you unconscious, foaming at the mouth on the floor. They found out about your habit and fired you."

Candice sat stone-faced. Her stiff, dry, shoulder-length hair, frayed and split at the ends, was untamed under the sharp van light. Her sleepy-sad eyes stared lifelessly from one EMT to the other, then finally rested on the back windows of the ambulance. Car lights flashed from outside of her world. For a second, she wondered what life was like for those people out there—living their lives, not having to hold onto and deal with her problems. She was a product of molestation, rape, and assault. Placed in one abusive foster home after another. She eventually found herself floating through life, just like the song her mama used to sing, riding on a white cloud of something. A high that made it to Candice's adult world.

Just as quickly as Candice arrived at the hospital, she was discharged back to the streets, walking two miles home alone in the dark until she heard footsteps behind her. Slow jogging to a sprint. But when she turned around, no one was there. For years, she struggled with anxiety, so she just brushed it off. Removing the tape player from her pocket, she adjusted the headphones, increased the volume, and continued walking as the shadow followed behind.

Forty minutes later, Candice opened the door to the low-income one-bedroom vacancy she called home. She had only been there for a few weeks since leaving a shelter, where safety just didn't exist, especially for women. Candice moved back to the same apartment she had once lived in with her mother before she was sent away to live with strangers. She thought moving back would help with the healing process. *If I can see it, then I can face it,* she thought. But it didn't help. It just made her angrier, bitter, and shrink into what she told herself she would never become— her mother.

Flat-footed, she dragged her body to the only chair she owned and paused the song, staring dazedly into space. *I need to get my shit together,* she told herself, but it was just a matter of time. All it took was a few pills or a hit from some blow, and her shit would be together again. *It's nothing too serious,* she always convinced herself. But the truth hurts, and so do years of untreated depression and addiction. Now, she didn't have a job and would be put out on the streets, again. Candice raked her hands through her hair, pulling at the follicles.

Ahhhhh!

Her high-pitched scream went unnoticed and blended naturally with the other apartment tenants' chaos— stomping, crying, babies, and arguing. Candice cried into her hands as the shadow stretched across the darkening sky and draped over the apartment building.

Tap. Tap. Tap.

Pouring rain tapped and slapped against the bathroom window from outside. Seconds later, a slow drip quickly turned into a steady stream leaking from the unpatched hole in the ceiling due to poor maintenance inside the vacancy.

Sssssssss.

"Damn!" Candice whined, grimacing at the sound and sight of rainwater in her apartment. Wiping her wet face, she walked to the bathroom. The stream ran like a faucet onto the old hardwood floor. Briskly, Candice grabbed a mop bucket from under the kitchen sink, which her landlord had given her for times like this, not expecting what she saw inside the cabinet. She stared, watching it as it watched her. She never really planned to use it, but a woman who befriended her one night on the streets gave it to her, so she kept it.

"Just in case," said the woman with a nod.

Then, unlike any voice Candice had ever heard, a voice belonging to no one, spoke.

Do it, spoke the voice of many. *Don't you want to be happy like everyone else outside your world, Candice?*

The deep vibrational voice, dark and otherworldly, occupied the entire room, paralyzing Candice. Her eyes shifted wildly, searching for a person— any person— but no one was there but her.

41

Grab the syringe, Candice, instructed the voice. The apartment slowly rolled into darkness as the shadow filled the room, covering any form of light except for what stared back at Candice.

SNAP.

An invisible, weighty finger motioned the sound, tranquilizing Candice's body into white noise only she could hear.

Bzzzzzzzz.

Relax, spoke the haint. *No more stress. No more work. You hate responsibility. You hate answering to life. Answer to me— it's just you and me, Candice.* The deep, calm, and reassuring voice put Candice at ease in a trance-like state.

Tap. Tap. Tap.

The rain settled into Candice's ear, muting all other background noise, as she looked over to the bathroom window at the torrential downpour. Carefully, Candice grasped the liquid-filled, fixed-needle syringe, walked into the bathroom, and closed the door. The remaining pills she bought from a drug dealer up the street sat in the curve of the stained soap dish on the sink. She popped the remaining eight colorful pills in her mouth and ran water into the cup of her palm, washing down the drugs and swallowing hard. The shadow observed Candice.

Drawing a bath, Candice undressed, submerging herself under the warm running water, leaving her head resting on the rim of the tub. Reaching for the cassette player atop her clothes on the floor, she placed the headphones over her ears and pressed play before grabbing the needle next to it. The vein in the crease of her left arm throbbed from the tape the nurses at the hospital had wrapped around her arm just a couple of hours ago, before sending her off with discharge papers and no remedy for her problems. Attentively, she removed the flat cottonball, inserting the needle into the blue vein, releasing the liquid into her bloodstream. The drugs liquified her organs as the shadow suspended over her, releasing its legs like black strings waving in the windless room, turning the tub handle to the hottest water temperature. Its thin, wispy hairs, standing atop its ghastly sunken face, grinning at her.

Ease into it, Candice. Everything is going to be okay, reassured the voice— new music to her ears.

Closing her eyes, she slumped into the boiling hot water. Boils and blisters puffed her skin into red scalded flesh as white meat clumps formed all over her body and face from an overdose, drowning. She heard her heart beating under the water. Slow and hollow until it didn't anymore, lifting the black silhouette from the apartment, bringing night into day, and allowing Candice to ride and fly into a white death effortlessly.

Sloth
Proverbs 13:4
The soul of the sluggard desireth, and hath nothing:
but the soul of the diligent shall be made fat.

CHAPTER 9

The tour guide flipped the bathroom light switch, guiding the group to the kitchen.

"With a few minor updates over the years, a great deal of scrumptious meals have been prepared and eaten in this very kitchen." Smiling, she continued. "Can't you just imagine the feasts?!" Closing her eyes, she sucked her teeth as though she could taste the food. "But did you know too much of a good thing is bad for you, and too much of a bad thing could *kill* you?"

The friends glanced at each other, taken aback, unsure what she meant.

"1 Corinthians 6:19," the tour guide continued, eyeing the kitchen as though investigating something unseen. "Your body is your temple," she said, her voice trailing off. "That's what they tried to explain to Paisley. But she chose not to listen. Isn't that right, Paisley?"

CHAPTER 10
2024

"Did you see the lineup?" Paisley asked her brother, scrolling on her phone at the bus stop.

"Not yet," said Shawn. "But I saw a post about them rescheduling the grand opening of the new *Sugar Shack* by us next week, so you know what that means." A slow smile crept upon Shawn's face as he raised his eyebrows, rubbing his hands together, shaking his head, and licking his lips.

"It's about to be *on!*" said Paisley, celebrating with a seated dance. She returned her attention to her phone. "Ooh! Look what they havin' next week!" Paisley lifted her phone, showing her brother as they read the upcoming weekly special together:

Carmel Apple Butter Cookie
Candied Yams A La Mode
Peanut Butter Crunch Cake Cookie
Pineapple Upside Down Coconut Layer Cake Cookie
Kentucky Bourbon Brownie Batter

"This menu's *killing* the game!" said Paisley. "I'm goin' next week— I'm not missin' this special for nothin'!"

∽

It was a Friday morning school day when Paisley noticed her clothes fitting smaller than usual.

"Ugh!" she huffed, examining herself in the mirror. Paisley's skin was the hue of golden sand, and her body was a healthy, shapely medium. Yet, she struggled immensely with her eating habits and compared herself to unrealistic edited photos of random strangers online. Unsatisfied with her body, she searched her laundry bin for a larger shirt and pants, but found none, leaving her physically uncomfortable but ordinarily hungry for breakfast.

Downstairs in the kitchen, Shawn and Dad sat at the round dining table doing separate things. Shawn listened to music with headphones hanging off his head while eating a bacon, egg, and cheese breakfast sandwich. Dad read a business brief over a plate of crumbs while drinking an espresso. Mom prepared the last breakfast sandwich over the stove.

"Good Morning!" said Paisley, melodically. She made her rounds, kissing her father on the cheek, hugging her brother around the neck, shifting his headphones, and rushing to the refrigerator for the last gulp of orange juice.

"Well, good morning to you, too, Miss Missy," greeted her mother with a smile. Paisley held the carton, leaning to kiss her mother's cheek, and grabbed the plated sandwich with the other hand. Standing while eating at the kitchen island, her mother gave her the "Mama look."

"Hold up," said her mother, evaluating Paisley. "Those pants are fitting a bit too tightly." Paisley's mom squinted, examining her daughter's physique for a better look. Then she bent backward, with magnified eyes at her daughter's backside.

Paisley's dad looked quizzically at his daughter from above his report and glasses. "You ain't wearing *that* out *there* for some raggedy lil' boy to be lookin' at you. Go on back upstairs and change." Glancing at his wife, smirking, he placed the report back over his eyes.

"Please, stop!" Paisley put her hand across her face, embarrassed, but laughing too. "I gotta do my laundry."

Then, Shawn had to chime in, egging it on as he stuffed his face. "I keep telling her," Shawn said casually between big bites, short breaths, swallowing hard, clearing his throat, and sucking his teeth. "If she keeps going to *Sugar Shack*, she gon' turn into *Sugar Shack*."

"Stop teasing your sister," said their father with a serious tone, his eyes sitting above the report again.

Their mother playfully threw the kitchen towel at Shawn, pointing at him with a hidden smile in her eyes. "Boy, hush! And eat with your mouth closed for once!"

Straightening her face and getting serious, her eyes softened as she chose her words carefully not to offend her daughter. "There is *some* truth to what your brother is saying. You need to *slow down* on those sweets, baby. I don't want you getting sick— like last time. Remember, your body is fragile."

Paisley knew exactly what her mother was alluding to. She had OCD— Obsessive-Compulsive Disorder and had previously struggled with an eating disorder— overeating, bingeing, or gorging herself, only to purge her food up later for the fear of gaining weight. *Body dysmorphia* was the diagnosis.

Paisley was admitted by ambulance to the hospital for an emergency surgery, not once but twice, as a teenager. And although she was under anesthesia, she lay awake with semi-paralysis on the operating table as the shadow crouched, lurking in the corner of the wall, speaking in an indistinct, distant language. Grinning. Staring. Watching. Waiting.

With open eyes, Paisley watched the doctors dissect her with shiny, sharp metal instruments under a microscope of screeching white spotlights.

"Alright, y'all," said Paisley, not wanting to think or talk about it. "I get it."

Noticing her agitation, her mom hugged Paisley, smothering her with motherly love, affection, and comforting words she needed. "Baby, I promise, we are not trying to hurt your feelings or cause you to go down a dark path with this. We just worry about you. We love you and care about you. That's all."

"I know," said Paisley, leaning into her mother's arms. "I will– I promise. I'll slow down."

Paisley's family let it go and returned to their regular morning conversations, but Paisley still felt the sting of the family talk. Brushing off the bad memories of "that time" in her life, she finished her breakfast, said her goodbyes, and headed out the door to catch the school bus with her brother. But Shawn continued to get on her case even on the bus.

"You need to slow down, sis," said Shawn. "I know you like eating there— I get it. I do too. But you've been there every day this week and last week buying the whole line-up. And you're trynna go again, next week. That's a lot on you after everything. We're worried about you and don't want the same thing to happen again."

Shrugging, Paisley looked away, ignoring her brother the rest of the ride to school.

At school, Paisley couldn't take her mind off the weekly special as she sat behind her desk. So, when the teacher turned his back to write on the board, Paisley uncovered her phone and did a quick search, and there it was— the post about the new *Sugar Shack* grand opening near her house. *I'm not missing this*, she told herself.

Paisley enjoyed watching and listening to people eat. Chewing, licking, slurping, and burping into the camera's microphone was utterly satisfying to her. That was ASMR— Autonomous Sensory Meridian Response.

Paisley and millions of other viewers experienced this gratification through the senses and eyes. Desire. Fantasy. Teasing the taste buds. Digesting bright images and loud sounds. And even better— no calories— a foodies dream.

She scrolled until she came across the post of the new *Sugar Shack* location near her home. They were promoting the grand opening and talking about a new feature to the event: a *Wall of Fame*. A young woman wearing the infamous mint green *Sugar Shack* hat and t-shirt spoke energetically into the camera on the video post that quickly garnered thousands of viewers.

"To win the competition, one lucky person will have to eat the weekly special 20 times within 30 minutes! Do the math, guys— that's 100 whopping *Sugar Shacks!* And guess what? We will come to you. That's right! You don't even have to leave your house. We will bring the *Sugar Shack* to your home for foodies like you to indulge and watch the next *Sugar Shack Super Star* in all their glory, and the treat is on us! So, come on down and enter to win the chance of becoming our first *Sugar Shack Champ*, and get your picture on our *Wall of Fame!*"

Paisley imagined her face on the *Sugar Shack Wall of Fame* for eating those delicious, delectable, decadent, scrumptious, mouth-watering cookies.

All for me and all for free, she thought, smiling and envisioning her face in the framed photo on the wall.

❧

Finally, it was the weekend.

"We're leaving for revival!" yelled Paisley's mother from downstairs at the 'front door. "Are you dressed yet?"

Paisley dramatically held her stomach, falling on her bed. "My stomach hurts," she lied. "I'm gonna rest here until y'all get back." *I'll pray for forgiveness later,* she thought to herself.

"Okay, sweetness— just take it easy and don't forget to take your medication. We'll be back in a few hours— I'll call you when we're on our way back home. And let me know if you need anything while we're out, okay?"

"Okay," said Paisley, feeling bad for lying. She tried to smooth it over. "Thank you, Mom. I love you."

"I love you too, sweetheart— be back in a few."

When Paisley finally heard the door close, she called *Sugar Shack* to enter the competition.

She had a few hours left before the family returned from church.

The media crew set up cameras, and *Sugar Shack* employees carried tall, mint green boxes of the weekly lineup by the droves, filling the entire kitchen island counter.

Sitting at the kitchen island, Paisley didn't realize how many people would come by the house. Every time she ate a cookie, there seemed to be ten more people arriving, holding their camera phones to capture the whole thing. Some faces she recognized from watching their viral ASMR videos. When she started slowing down, motivation from her favorite influencers gave Paisley the extra boost of confidence she needed to keep going.

Paisley swallowed the cookies as a dark black cloud rolled into the sunlit sky, dimming the light that only Paisley noticed, but she kept eating. The room grew humid and stuffy as she ate cookie after cookie, one by one, leaving empty boxes tumbling from the towering stacks, bringing a primitive voice to her ear.

Keep going. You're almost there, encouraged the abysmal voice from nowhere. *You can't stop now.*

Paisley heard it before in the hospital, both times, on the operating table. They had to stitch her stomach from the hole that burned itself into her intestines.

The body-less voice continued, *You've come too far. Champs don't quit what they love.*

At cookie number eighty-two, her intestines began tearing apart like a cotton sheet separated by bare hands, but Paisley kept eating. Heat. Entrapped in the prison of her own body, Paisley was a small rocky boat in a riptide current before shipwreck. Unraveling, drowning– washing away to the empty sea floor. In a spin of dizziness, her intestinal stitches slowly, detaching, stretching wider and broader, shredding, and stretching deep within.

Eating cookie after cookie, her cheeks swollen and fat, a dark shadow moved in the left corner of her eyes as she choked. The spirit appeared as it had before. But this time, it brought itself to the light.

The dark shadow inches away from her face. Watching and staring into her eyes from a faraway land. And as she searched the room, the demon's smiling face shone on each person. Around her. Behind her. In front of her. Overtop of her. Its large smile, stretching wider.

Gasping for breath, Paisley kept eating. The spirit, feeding as well. Like the animal it was. Smelling her hair, licking her swollen, stuffed cheeks. Her inner screams, invisible to the crowd, met with laughter—concealed torture— a hell in her own body.

Suffocating trapped food in her esophagus, busting the seams of her large and small intestines. And then the purge, lodged in her engorged throat, strangling her. Paisley silently choked. Drowning in her own bile.

Keep going, the voice pressed her. *This is your chance. Don't give up.*

People gathered, crowding the front lawn, eating a complimentary cookie, taking pictures, and watching the livestream. Unaware of the spectacle inside, they laughed as people ran out of the house, until an ambulance arrived, carrying a sheet-covered body on a stretcher out the front door through the crowd. A broadcast journalist covered the breaking news.

> "A young woman has died in the middle of 1.3 million viewers, in person and online, who watched the competition until she fed herself to death all for the infamous *Sugar Shack* cookies. We will have more on the scene of this fatal incident as the story develops. Reporting live on the scene. I'm Gabriela Rodriguez."

The autopsy report disclosed: "Death by gastric rupture from overconsumption." But the final say came from the hashtag ASMR followers who would later replay the reposted videos as a viral trend, memorializing Candice as the most infamous *Sugar Shack Champ* on the *Wall of Fame*.

Vrrr. Vrrr. Vrrr. Vrrr. Vrrr. Vrr.

Paisley's phone vibrated as her mother's call went unanswered.

Gluttony
Proverbs 23:20-21

Be not among winebibbers; among riotous eaters of flesh:
For the drunkard and the glutton shall come to poverty:
and drowsiness shall clothe a man with rags.

CHAPTER 11

"Even too much of a good thing is bad for you," said the tour guide, walking to the kitchen window overlooking a small cottage covered in honeysuckle and Morning glories. "The garden house is right this way." The tour guide led the group through a back door to the small house.

"The garden house was once the slave quarters. Rumor has it that Master Charles Le Rue de Baptiste bore a child with one of his house slaves who would later haunt the property. But, then again, what are ghost stories other than fables crafted by fear?"

Ignoring the question, Chelsea nudged Evalina, pointing to a man in a picture frame on the wall. The tour guide quickly caught wind of their favorable expressions.

"Oh, I see," said the tour guide. "You have found, Giovanni. He *is* quite easy on the eyes— if I may say so, myself."

"Who is *he*?" asked Chelsea, ogling at the alluring, tall, dark, and handsome chiseled man with the hairless face, strong jawline, light green eyes, thick, naturally arched jet-black eyebrows, low wavy fade, and the sculpted physique of a Greek God.

"That is the exact question he hoped people would ask," began the tour guide, turning to the group. "To Giovanni, he was perfectly perfect, especially on his own."

CHAPTER 12
2017

"I'm out here pumping iron, man!" Giovanni gloated, partially succeeding in lifting a 275-pound weight from his chest to the rack. "You ain't 'bout this life."

Creed made a face, spotting him at the bar. "What you know bout *that* life? You out here strugglin'— you betta chill the hell out before ya hurt ya self."

"Bruh, I'm good!" said Giovanni, sitting up on the bench. "A spotter— for what? I'm handlin' mines."

"Yeah. Okay," Creed smirked sarcastically. "Look, dawg, I'm just trynna help. But I see you *got* this. So, coo." He stepped back, gesturing his hands off.

Giovanni lay back on the bench, gripping the weight bar again with newfound confidence. Straining, he brought the weight to his chest, then back up to the rack before exhaling in relief and sitting up. "That's right. I got this, and don't you forget it," said Giovanni, laughing arrogantly. "I mean, when you look *this* good, got the followers *I* got, the ultimate man cave gym, the girls— come on man— you'd be as good as me too, but until then, enjoy sittin' on the sidelines— my brotha."

Giovanni was a second-generation immigrant, with sea-green eyes inherited from his Sicilian father and dark features from his Somali mother. Staring in the mirror, he pinched his chin, looking from left to right with a smug smile, and air-kissed himself.

"Wow!" said Creed. I didn't know you were this narcissistic and cocky— you suh-muh-muh-bish!"

They fell out laughing.

"You know it's true— I mean, what can I say— I'm *him*," Giovanni admired his best practiced smile in the mirror before getting a good laugh. "Naw, but for real, man. All jokes aside. This is it." Giovanni elongated his arms as though he were displaying a grand prize. "I worked hard for this— I mean, granted, I didn't *buy* the main house, but at least I'm renting the guest house."

"Yeah," said Creed, shaking his head. "This place *is* sick. And truth be told, man— I really didn't think you could pull it off, but you did. Surprised the hell outta me!"

Giovanni grinned proudly, flexing his muscles in the mirror, admiring the work of art that had granted him a semi-professional modeling career and 29k followers— and counting—all thanks to his good looks and sexually suggestive poses.

Creed had grown accustomed to Giovanni's conceited ways throughout the years as his best friend, but this level of arrogance was becoming a bit extreme, even for him. So, like the good friend he was, Creed attempted to impart some wisdom, quoting from the Bible. "'The wicked, through the pride of his countenance, will not seek after God: God is not in all his thoughts.'" Creed continued, "Man, you betta recognize and give God the credit. Stop thinkin' you out here doin' things on ya own and by ya self."

"Aww, so now you're religious?" asked Giovanni, mocking Creed.

"Look, I ain't no saint by any stretch of the imagination, but I know a thing or two about the Bible. And you should too."

"Well, that ain't for me," said Giovanni, walking away. "So, leave that Bible talk over there." He pointed to the door.

"Look, man," said Creed, irritated. "Do what you wanna do. I gotta shake anyway. I promised to take my girl on a lil' lunch date, so I'll hit you lata."

"Aight," said Giovanni, walking to Creed for their special choreographed handshake. "And don't forget to give Serenity a kiss for me, too," he joked, snickering.

"Oh. Okay, okay. I see how it is," said Creed, nodding with a smirk. "She might have liked you when we were kids, but she chose me."

They had one final laugh before Creed motioned a lazy salute from his forehead, heading to the car. "Lata, man."

Giovanni increased the volume on his wireless headphones, beginning his typical daily routine of meal prep, eating, and an intense workout:

- ✓ *8 raw eggs*
- ✓ *250 grams of protein powder in a high-protein shake, steak, grilled chicken, and asparagus.*
- ✓ *5 energy drinks*
- ✓ *2 lines of cocaine*
- ✓ *And injectable steroids*

Dancing in the mirror— popping, locking, and krumping— gliding his feet across the floor and spinning smoothly, flexing his six-pack abs, and bouncing his chest muscles, he vibed out.

Arm day consisted of four sets of ten, adding heavy lifts, calisthenics— push-ups and chin-ups— and abdominal vacuums into the plan, maintaining his V cut. And of course, a strong final pump to be 100 percent camera-ready.

"Let's do this, baby! It's showtime!" Giovanni cheered, beating on his chest as though he had a full audience instead of just one— himself. This time, he would show his followers, all the people who idolized him worldwide, his heaviest bench press. Giovanni grabbed his phone from the counter, got his best flex on, and turned on the livestream, talking directly into the camera.

"400-pound weight lift on bar, baby! Yeah, that's right. Ya boy is about to show all these wannabes out here who the real man is!" The livestream moved in numbers from 151 to 27k followers. Giovanni smiled sideways, staring at the increasing numbers while downing his last energy drink.

"Ya boy is living the dream— 400 pounds baby! Who's pushing this kind of weight looking as good as me, huh?!" He pointed into the camera. "This is a new one for all y'all who doubted me!"

The livestream chat was insane with his fans' comments in real-time:

Giovanni set the phone against the mirror for the perfect view and angle before stretching his arms and back, cracking his neck from side to side, and sitting on the weight bench. Flattening his back on the bench with knees bent and feet shoulder-width apart against the newly remodeled epoxy gloss floor, he slightly lifted his head to view the livestream. Emoji hearts, muscles, and clapping hands encircled his reflection in the video.

"Hell yeah," Giovanni said aloud, until fear crept in. This was his first time attacking a lift of this magnitude. Nevertheless, with a little internal pep talk, he smiled. *I got this. This is all me.*

Lying back on the bench, Giovanni gripped the barbell, removing it from the rack and lifting it above his chest perpendicularly. Straining, he lowered the bar to his chest. With every ounce of strength, he lifted the bar in full extension. *One,* he counted to himself. But he couldn't just let one be it— the end-all be-all. *I can do two more,* he coached himself. Lowering the bar slowly back down to his chest, heat pressure-packed around his head, arms, and chest as he strained, raising the bar in full extension. *Two.*

As Giovanni began the third and final lift, the dark presence emerged over the cottage, entering the house gym, blackening the walls and the windows. Giovanni looked to his left at the window he could no longer see through. Mystified, he returned his attention to the weight. Lowering the bar to his chest, pressure pulled at his muscles as his eyes bulged and the veins in his forehead fattened. And that is when he heard the warped voice of no one, silencing the music.

What are you waiting for? It said. *You have more in you. Remember, you need no one.*

Giovanni stiffened in panic, stretching his eyes around the room, straining to hold the weight bar. He was the only person in the room. Attempting to push the bar away from his chest, Giovanni's hands slipped, shifting the weight bar to his neck.

"Ahh!" he cried out in anguish. Tears— pushing from his eyes. Saliva— spurting from his lips. Pressing and straining as hard as he could against the weight bar, the unbalanced weight lowered against his neck.

Struggling to maneuver the weight, the shadow emerged crouching on top of him. The black silhouette of long, knuckly hands wrapped around Giovanni's fists, clutching the bar and forcing 400 pounds of weight against Giovanni's neck, choking, crushing, and severing his head from his body in the grave pursuit of perfection.

Pride
Proverbs 16:18
Pride goeth before destruction, and an haughty spirit before a fall.

CHAPTER 13

"Giovanni was perfectly perfect on his own, and quite invincible… so he thought," said the tour guide, closing the door to the garden house. "Come with me." She led the group back to the house, where they walked through the long hallway covered in a mosaic of gold-framed people until they entered a lavish library.

"This beautiful study was built from the sugar maple trees on this property. Isn't the woodwork just splendid? It was built for a businessman like Patrick, an executive. He had the cars. Designer clothes. Jewelry. But most importantly, he had the promotions. But even with an increase, there is always a price to pay."

Jamison interrupted, "'To whom much is given, much will be required.' Luke 12:48." He shrugged, forcing a polite grin. "My father's a pastor."

"Ah, yes, a preacher's kid," said the tour guide, flashing her eyes then fixating on something far away. "At what cost would you give *your* life? That was Patrick's dilemma."

CHAPTER 14
1999

When you get the money, you get the power. Then, the world is yours— that was Patrick's motto. The corporate sector was Patrick's sole love, and that love granted him money and power. He was a taker. But you wouldn't have known it from the likes of his public persona. He donated to charities. He sat on respectable Boards. He dined with the wealthy. All he ever wanted was at his fingertips.

Patrick, clove brown, was tall and lanky with a low, even haircut. Growing up, taller than his peers, he bullied kids around him, believing he was better than everyone, which would later carry over into adulthood, but not without direct lessons from his father.

Patrick learned from the best. One day, after a long church service, his father, Pastor Miller, had a "sit-down" with him about life. Dressed in his usual long, bulky crimson robe, his father sat in the preacher's throne-inspired seat in the pulpit overlooking empty pews.

"The strategy, son, is to learn what they love and become that," he explained. "It's all in how you spin the story. Some call it sleight of hand. Others call it manipulation. No matter the name, it all gives you money and power. And that's what this life on earth is all about. You hear me, son?"

"Yes, sir," replied young Patrick.

Glaring at his son under the fluorescent church lights, Pastor Miller clutched his son's shoulder, reiterating. "Get them to love you first, then you get all the power you need. Think real hard about that." Standing up, Pastor Miller exited the church, leaving his son by himself staring at the vibrant stained glass windows of Jesus on the cross.

Throughout his adolescence, Patrick watched his father teach him the ins and outs of criminal behavior— how to get money illegally from the one place no one would ask questions: the church.

Pastor Miller of New Bethel Baptist Church of God, and a tele-evangelist with a special on the 2:00 a.m. local television network, threw sprinkles of water on the faces of women and men who'd fall out "in the spirit" as though they needed an exorcism to bring them back.

He'd guilt-trip congregants to stand in a line at the altar to give their last dollar, over the amount they could realistically afford. He stole from the tithes and offerings collection plates, funding his selfish habits, adulterous affairs, and family life with jet-setting travel excursions, a celebrity lifestyle, and worldly possessions. He was a criminal. A crooked, conniving, Bible-toting thief, who reaped the barren fruit of his sins. He was wayward, teaching his son the way of a sinful world.

Patrick got his criminal mind easily and got off easier, with Pastor Miller responsible for digging Patrick out of the holes he had dug for himself. He made sure his son's name was scrubbed squeaky clean and cleared despite Patrick's carelessness that would, in due time, convert his juvenile delinquency to white-collar crime.

However, young Patrick's uncontrollable behavior became more difficult for his mother to handle, so she sent him to her grandmother's house in rural Kentucky during the summer.

Patrick's great-grandmother— a sweet, God-fearing woman— always took time to instill morals and values into his life. Her lessons, based on wise teachings from the Bible, were taught from love and not lies.

"You got to make better choices," instructed his great-grandmother. "I don't want nothin' bad happenin' to you. Pray and read ya Bible, baby. Get to know Jesus for ya self. You hear me, chil'?"

"Yes, ma'am," replied young Patrick.

Patrick's great-grandmother hugged him tightly, wrapping him in her strong arms. "Alright. Now, go on, git." Smiling, she shooed him upstairs. "Need to make a phone call right quick, that you don't need to hear."

Young Patrick made his way up the carpeted staircase, but stopped at the top step to sit and eavesdrop on grown folks' conversation.

"Baby, I'm not trynna get in ya business," she explained to Patrick's mother, "but you need to leave that husband of yours. He is not raisin' Patrick in a Godly fashion, and based on what I'm hearin' through the grapevine, he ain't much of a husband either—

or pastor." Then, like she always did, she concluded with a verse from the Bible: "'He that spareth his rod hateth his son: but he that loveth him chasteneth him betimes.' You need to read Proverbs 13:24, baby. Listen to me. I love you."

Although Patrick's mother was provoked to leave her husband, she never did. She didn't like or agree with how her husband lived or the lessons he taught Patrick, but she benefited from the lifestyle. And when Patrick's great-grandmother passed away, the wise lessons she shared became harder to hear and eventually faded from his memory. But some things in Patrick's life remained clear—his father's lessons of using the church for deception, trickery, and subterfuge—all false pretenses. And despite Pastor Miller's stealing, lying, and even murder, he died a saint to many and a devil to others. However, while Patrick had some fame, he didn't have the same fortune.

"Job well done, Patrick. You've earned the promotion," announced Scott Briscoe, the President of Nitrex Oil Company Inc. While the executive team congratulated Patrick, his direct co-workers gossiped in the tight corners of their shared office.

"Watch out for *him*," whispered Bridgette, huddled with other co-workers, leaning over a table. "He's known to *screw* people over."

"Yeah," agreed William, rolling his eyes and snapping his neck expressively, enunciating each syllable. "Tell me about it. I've heard he will rob Peter to pay Paul, to fund *Patrick*." The musical way he said Patrick's name made everyone snicker as they shifted their gaze to the glass-enclosed office.

Patrick smiled for a photo, holding a black and gold plaque in one hand and shaking the hand of the company President in the other.

William returned his narrow-hooded eyes to the huddle, wincing with each distinct vowel extension, displaying his bottom teeth as he spoke, "He'll step on *anyone's* neck to get to the top."

Patrick's co-workers quietly ragged on him as he accepted his new title as CFO—Chief Financial Officer. Viewed as "covetous" and "selfish" by co-workers, he believed those traits led to success. Say, if one of his colleagues he viewed as inferior or below him shared an unacknowledged idea, Patrick would repeat the idea verbatim, taking credit and praise as though he had won the Nobel Peace Prize. He was well-liked by higher-ups but despised by colleagues he considered "subordinates."

No matter what it took, acquiring more money and power was his MO. And manipulation was his specialty, especially when fluctuating numbers and forging signatures— all fraud.

One night, Patrick was the last person in the high-rise building besides the first-floor security guard. Sitting in his dark office on the top floor, his laptop lit up the room, intensifying the lines on his face as he changed the numbers in the account of the company's largest client, transferring the funds to his personal account.

They won't miss it, he thought. "Sometimes you've got to cheat to win," he mumbled, clicking the submit tab. The extra zeros made his account way more impressive than he imagined. *The ideal end to a busy day,* Patrick thought. He closed the lid to his laptop, leaving the office.

Driving to his condo, remorse crept in, convicting Patrick to second-guess his decision. "What the hell did I just do?" Then, spasmodically, he turned up the music on the radio and switched his perspective. "No, I'm good," he said, soothing himself. "They'll *never* notice. It's just a couple of missing zeros— they're swimming in money."

Arriving home, Patrick prepared for a peaceful night. Showering behind the steamy glass doors, the shadow levitated over the house. Enfolding the balconies and porch like a blanket. Fingering the wind chimes and entering the open bathroom window of the condo. Watching.

The next morning, Patrick's phone was blowing up. All urgent voicemail— unanswered and text messages— unread. And when he opened his computer, the screen was locked. It was over— just like that. But this time, no one was there to clean and clear his name.

Coming to terms with the extent of the error— the grave mistake— he sat with his mindless mind in darkness. Squeezing him into the past— the memories— buried and resurrected, narrowing the walls. A circus of clowns laughed in his face. Patrick peeked out the window blinds from his office. The FBI and SWAT surrounded the house, guns drawn. Flashing lights peeking through the blinds— the colors of America and its dream left him disoriented while gazing out the window.

Shutting the blinds, he sat in his office chair. Peering past the room, his deceased maternal great-grandmother appeared alive again, after all those years, sitting on her favorite plastic-covered couch. Her smiling face, comfort, and hope under the mask of a doomed reality altered to a frown.

Take yourself out, baby. Her distorted lips, speaking from a deep, split voice that wasn't hers. *That's the only way.*

His great-grandmother never would have spoken those words. But this one did. Her face— melting and glitching from smile to frown to smile. Her skin— dripping, burning holes into the plastic. Patrick's mind spun faster, caving in on itself. Glancing at his phone, Patrick had a missed call and a voice message from his financial advisor.

"Patrick! Call me immediately! What's going on?! What has happened?!"

Patrick pressed the power button. It was over, but he was not going to prison.

"Do what you gotta do to escape purgatory before hell," he recalled hearing a friend say. Then, he heard another voice.

Keep your cool, Patrick. We've known each other a long while. Its deep voice vibrated, stretching the walls. *This is your chance to leave it all behind.*

Standing on the chair, Patrick grabbed his pants-length tie, wrapped it, and double-knotted it around the rod. Closing his eyes, he gingerly slid his feet from the fringe of the office chair, breaking his neck. His body convulsed, swaying as the fan was designed.

Greed
1 Timothy 6:10

For the love of money is the root of all evil: which, while some coveted after, they have erred from the faith, and pierced themselves through with many sorrows.

CHAPTER 15

"I guess you can say it was professional suicide for Patrick," said the tour guide, turning off the light and walking out of the office.

The group, uneasy and staring at the ceiling fan, anxiously followed behind the tour guide up the grand staircase and through the hallway to enter a guest bedroom. A framed picture of two women hung on the wall with the words "besties" engraved.

"They were best friends," explained the tour guide. "Like sisters, they were close. There were signs— early on— that were disregarded. Benefit of the doubt, I suppose. But when someone shows you who they are, believe them."

CHAPTER 16
2019

"That's my best frannn!" Iyana sang, laughing while taking a picture with Nikki.

Iyana was what many described as "high yella." The complexion of butter-browned cornbread, nicknamed "baby girl" by family and "spoiled" by haters. Dressed in high fashion, she wore the latest hairstyles with swooped and slicked baby hair framing her dollface.

Nikki was more laid back and low-maintenance. She didn't have parents funding everything for her. Her mother had passed when she was thirteen, leaving her with her father's negligent side. Her skin, caramelized brown. With her oval goddess face, outlined by a colorful headwrap, she was considered "Afrocentric" or very in touch with her roots.

Iyana removed the photo from the vintage camera, shaking the picture until their image emerged.

"That's cute, sis," said Nikki. "But you know what they say. Keep your friends close and your enemies closer— that's biblical."

"Girl, stop!" said Iyana, laughing, doubling over. "You got my sides hurtin'! That is *not* in the Bible!"

"True, but you've gotta admit— it's a good quote," said Nikki.

They both laughed. That was their thing. They were BFFs.

"Girl, your man is *so* sexy!" Nikki leaned back, laughing. "You've got to tell me *all* about him."

"He's cool," said Iyana flatly. She wanted to keep her new relationship private. But Nikki kept probing.

"Girl, what's he *like*?!"

"Nothing major," Iyana said, not wanting Ray to become the center of attention in their friendship. "We're getting to know each other." Iyana knew how Nikki could get when she got a new friend or boyfriend— she could get in her feelings, wanting to be reminded that *she* was the best friend and no one else.

"Girl, I know you're all private and secretive, but you need to spill the beans," said Nikki.

"Look, I don't wanna jinx it," said Iyana. "Things are going pretty well for us right now, so I don't wanna mess things up by talking about him too soon."

"My bad, sis, I'm sorry," said Nikki sympathetically, matching Iyana's energy. "Sis, if it makes you feel any better, I won't say anything else about fine-ass Ray, okay– mums the word. I promise." Nikki acted like she was zipping her lips with a silly grin.

"Okay, good," said Iyana, joining in the laugh.

"So, how is *it*?" asked Nikki, breaking her promise. "'Cause when you get done with him, you can just pass him right on over here to me!"

"Girl— Stop! I'm not answering any more questions about Ray– and you done went too far— change the subject!" Iyana snapped a pillow at Nikki, who held it over her face, concealing a sneaky smile.

While it was a joke, when Iyana got home, she couldn't deny the feeling. Some things were just off limits to even the best of friends. But Nikki didn't seem to get the picture, which ultimately got under Iyana's skin.

Weeks passed, and Nikki's behavior became stranger to Iyana. Nikki started dressing like her, wearing her hair the same way, and changing her interests based on what Iyana liked. She randomly popped up at places she expected to see Iyana and Ray together. Even when Nikki and Iyana hung out, and Ray was around, Nikki competed for Ray's attention, always siding with him over Iyana during heated debates and oversharing personal information. She was getting too close for comfort.

Ray noticed the change in Nikki as well. "I don't know what's up with ya friend, but it seems like she's trynna be like you. It's like she wants to *be* you or something," Ray said, shaking his head. "Be careful around her. I don't trust her... There's something about her— I don't know, but just be careful, babe."

And as time passed, Nikki became more needy and dependent on Iyana.

"She's jealous," Iyana's mother clarified, styling her hair with the curling iron. "You better watch out for her, baby. I never really liked that girl, nohow. Why do you even hang out with her? She's always been too clingy and controlling. Why can't you see that? And I see how she dresses like you. Baby, that's someone who's trynna secretly *be* you. Don't you see her competing with you? I can see right through that lil' girl— she's trynna outdo you. That's envy." Iyana's mama placed the hot iron on a plate, giving her full attention. "Don't forget, baby, a smile is really just a frown turned upside down. *Watch* her."

The advice from her mother and boyfriend, lay thick on Iyana's mind. *They're right*, she thought. Then, another thought followed. *I don't trust Nikki.* So, to remedy the issue, Iyana took a break from Nikki and hung out with some other friends.

Nikki sensed the change. It had been days since she heard from Iyana, who was unavailable and unresponsive to her texts and calls.

"I'm just hanging with some friends this weekend," said Iyana when Nikki finally got a hold of her.

Nikki knew what was happening— Iyana was ghosting her, creating distance, fueling Nikki's anger and possessiveness. So, after a couple of days of not hearing from Iyana, Nikki dialed her number to bring their "sisterly" bond back into full gear.

"Let's just hang together at the park," said Nikki over the phone. "It's so much better when it's just the two of us— like old times."

Iyana wasn't feeling the conversation or ready to address the situation, especially since she couldn't shake the tinge of jealousy she sensed in Nikki. But she pushed aside her reluctance. "That's cool," said Iyana, hesitantly. "Meet you at the trail at 5:30 pm at our usual spot in an hour?"

"Yep, I'll be there," said Nikki. "See you in a bit."

Hanging up the phone, Nikki returned to a make-shift altar she built for her and Iyana's friendship. She set a photo of Iyana in the middle. Sitting on her knees, Nikki laid a stone slab on the floor before her, lighting three candles. A white candle for purity. A pink candle for affection and friendship, and a red candle for passion and love. For potency, she drizzled the candles with local pure raw honey from Kentucky bees to attract sweetness and a renewed friendship.

Nikki wrote Iyana's name on a small piece of papyrus cloth and pinned a photo of her and Iyana. Folding the fabric into four squares representing the four cardinal directions and four seasons, Nikki placed the items into a muslin sachet containing an assortment of herbs— rosemary sprig, a small quartz crystal, and violet petals layered in rose and cinnamon oils to enhance the curse.

Tying a knot in the sachet, she placed the ribbons of the string around her fingers like a rosary and closed her eyes, praying with intention. Summoning— in a distant indigenous language passed down in her family. Calling forth the spirit guides. The candle flames burned brighter and higher on the altar, waving and flickering. "Ashe," she whispered, sealing the prayer and opening her eyes. And as she watched the flame heighten, uniting all three candles into one light, a figureless shadow entered the room. Watching her, too.

Walking along the trail, Nikki combed her fingers through Iyana's hair.

"Girl— I just love your hair. What products do you use?" Nikki collected three loose hair strands from the back of Iyana's shirt.

"Just some leave-in conditioner is all," said Iyana, rolling her loose ponytail into a ball behind her head, recalling the cautionary advice from her mother and boyfriend. "Alright," said Iyana, stretching her legs and arms. "Ten more minutes left to run this stretch until dark, then I'll have to call it a night." Iyana went into a full sprint, hoping to leave Nikki in the dust.

"Let's finish strong, sis," said Nikki. Pushing the hair strands deep into her pocket, she picked up the pace to catch up to Iyana.

Arriving home from the park, Nikki walked to the far treelined acreage behind the apartment building adjacent to the river. Inspecting the trees, she found the one she needed.

"There you are," she said. Touching and patting the trunk of the hackberry tree, she found a natural hole opening and placed Iyana's hair inside. Then, she stuffed the hole with small branches and soft mud from around the tree, repeating words she remembered her mother teaching her. Nikki stepped back, staring at the tree, admiring her work. "Three days' time, bestie," she whispered.

Walking in the open field to the house under the gleam of the white moon and a single bright star, the ancient spirit appeared floating through the sky, casting a black shadow over the rippling river current, and entered the apartment with Nikki.

A week had passed since Nikki had heard from Iyana. She wondered how things were going for her after the spell.

Vrrr. Vrrr.

Nikki's phone vibrated with Iyana's name and picture on the screen. "Just like clockwork," she said before answering the phone.

"Hey. We need to talk," said Iyana with a hint of aggravation.

Uh oh, thought Nikki. Iyana was not supposed to be mad. She was supposed to be *dying* to connect. *Maybe I didn't stuff the tree hole good enough. Damn.*

"Wassup, girl?" Nikki replied, worried and mentally backtracking her steps to the spell.

"It feels like we've both been kind of off lately," said Iyana. "We *never* argue or get into any fights, but I've been feeling something different between us. I really don't know how to explain it, but I feel it. Something is changing, and I really don't know what it is, but I just want you to know that I will *always* choose you over anyone and everyone, including Ray— I actually broke up with him this weekend."

Nikki finished the conversation with Iyana, pleased with herself. "Works like a charm," she laughed, ready for the next phase of the ritual.

The following day, Nikki invited Iyana over to her place. She needed her physically present and doped up. Iyana's aura– energy– spirit were required for this phase of the curse.

When Iyana arrived at Nikki's apartment, the aroma of burning sage and mint leaves saturated her nostrils. Closing her eyes, she slowly inhaled and exhaled the incense. And before Iyana knew it, she was wrapped in its rapture. Soaking in its magnetic fumes, tossing in its psychedelic kaleidoscope of colors, shapes, and textures. Lathering and penetrating her pores. Iyana collapsed, falling toward the floor. But Nikki caught her mid-fall and laid her across the blanket of the altar.

"Sis. Girl, wake up," said Nikki coldheartedly, sitting Iyana up from her side, talking into her face, and handling her roughly. She continued, shaking Iyana's shoulders and speaking without restraint, "I need you semi-woke at least— I can't stand your spoiled, high-maintenance ass."

Iyana opened her eyes with a faraway gaze. Gaining a modicum of consciousness, a wild, sluggish smile crept upon her lips.

"Good. Now stay," directed Nikki, releasing Iyana's shoulders and controlling her with words like a pet. Nikki returned her attention to the altar.

Iyana's distant stare remained. She looked out of her mind, staring out the side window into the abyss. Iyana watched the sunlight twinkle between the tree leaves, stripping her face into lines of white and cinnamon-brown.

The curse is growing stronger, Nikki thought, working the candle magic, flaring the flame. The shadow inched closer to Nikki. Watching.

That night, after taking Iyana home, Nikki sat at the altar of lit candles– a sanctuary of animal bones, gopher dust, moonstones, and burning sage.

She wrapped her hair in a fresh tight-knit cloth atop her head and began fixing the concoction the way her mama had taught her years ago. She had the power to heal or hurt people with plants— creating medicine, remedies, ointments, and potions.

The recipe— a family secret— was carried by the women in her family from West Africa to plantation life in the Americas. Nikki followed in their footsteps as a priestess and spiritualist—a practitioner of indigenous African animism, dating back to ancient African civilization.

Nikki recited the words from the spellbook written and bound by the hands of the ancestral women in her family, containing recipes, apothecary, history, and family trinkets and heirlooms that survived the holocaust of enslavement in the Americas. Much like all people of African descent enslaved on the distant land, Black culture was never destroyed by the atrocities of slavery, but survived, including Nikki's, or better yet, Nikita DeBois' family.

Nikki's ancestors were the enslaved Africans of Sacrée Plantation, as property of

Master Baptiste of France. Nikki was a direct descendant– a great-great-grandchild and offspring of one of the five biological children of Anna and Big John.

According to the book and oral narratives, Anna, a light-brown, slender house slave who kept the book hidden under her dress, secretly learned to read and write, allowing her to record her family history, recipes, Bible verses, and prayers. And while Anna wrote the book intentionally to do good and not harm, the person who possessed the book could choose to do either.

Consequently, as the book passed down in the family to different women with different experiences, each woman had a specific use for the book and contributed an entry, including a final section titled "Curses." When Nikki inherited the book from her mother, she chose the latter.

Conjuring a ruby potion wasn't white magic centered on positive vibes and energy work. It was a curse brewed from a recipe rooted in years of ancestral knowledge and antiquity. Generations of past stories told from one woman to the next. Now, she would carry on the family tradition as a vessel in veneration of her ancestors, so she thought.

Nikki concocted the mixture with five-day-old menstrual cramp blood soaked and wrung from a dirty pad she drained into a mason jar, combined with organic Kentucky honey, with notes of wildflowers and clover. The jar needed to be placed under Iyana's bed for one night of sleep during the brewing phase, prompting Iyana to desire only the likes of Nikki. *That's true loyalty,* thought Nikki. She just had to get the jar under Iyana's bed.

"Girls' night!" said Iyana, enthusiastic about having Nikki over.

She's coming back around, thought Nikki. The curse gradually worked, getting Iyana back to how she used to be— unaware of Nikki's ulterior motives.

After the movie ended, Nikki made her move. "Sis, I have to use the bathroom. I'll be right back." Closing the bathroom door, she removed the jar from her bag. Going through the usual routine of bathroom etiquette so as not to cause any suspicion, Nikki flushed the unused toilet bowl and ran water into the clean sink. Quietly, she opened the door and crept into Iyana's bedroom, softly placing the jar under her bed. Returning to the movie room, she yawned big, stretching her arms.

"Aight, sis," said Nikki. "I have to head home to get ready for work in the morning. It's getting late. Are y'all still having the get-together tomorrow evening at your house?"

"Just like every year," said Iyana, hugging Nikki. Get ya beauty sleep, so you can still have energy after work— and don't forget to BYOB!"

"I gotchu, sis. said Nikki. "See you tomorrow."

"Goodnight, sis," said Iyana. "See you later."

Nikki visited Iyana's house for the annual cookout and pool party. It was like a family reunion. Everyone was eating, line dancing, drinking, laughing, and having a good time. Nikki was glad that Iyana's mother was preoccupied with family visiting from out of town. Now, she didn't have to worry about being closely watched.

"Be right back," said Nikki. "I have to use the bathroom." She went into the house as though she was going to the bathroom. But instead, she walked into Iyana's bedroom, looked under the bed, and found the jar exactly where she had placed it the night before. Grabbing the jar, she put it in her shoulder bag and returned to the party.

"I'm back, girlie!" said Nikki, dancing and holding a red disposable cup at Iyana. "And look what I've brought? A BYOB to share. I made you a drink— with my special skills. You know I'm a mixologist."

Iyana had been day drinking and could barely stand straight. "Sis, take a seat and just look cute as you sip this," said Nikki.

Iyana drank the mixture and finished the cup in its entirety. "Ugh!" Iyana swallowed and coughed, doubling back and stumbling as she jolted over to vomit, but nothing came up— just dry heaves. Iyana had to live with what was now living inside of her. And it was working instantaneously.

Satisfactorily, Nikki delicately circle-rubbed Iyana's back and pulled loose hair strands behind her ear as she lay slumped over in her lap.

A few days later, the shadow emerged, cascading like curtains and dripping like warm ice cream over Nikki's building.

Ding dong.

Nikki scrunched her face in confusion, turning her head to look at the peephole-less door. *Who the hell could that be?* She didn't have plans with anyone or anybody besides herself and her spirit guides. "Who is it?"

"Sis, it's me— Iyana."

"Oh, my bad, girl! Here I come." Iyana typically called before coming over, but it didn't matter. She was *exactly* who she wanted to see. Iyana had the same idea.

"Hey, girl," said Iyana, walking into Nikki's apartment, letting in a couple of horse flies.

Iyana doesn't look so well, thought Nikki. She looked and smelled like death.

"Hey, girl," said Nikki, swatting flies and covering her nose. "What happened to you?" The overwhelming funk of sun-cooked garbage quickly congested the whole apartment. "What the hell's that smell?"

"Don't you just love it?" laughed Iyana. Her sunken eyes, darkening. Holding Nikki's shoulders with a death grip, the right side of Iyana's face drooped and sagged as something slid and puffed underneath, breaking the epidermis skin barrier. Small white worms wiggled and bubbled free from blood-pus saturated sores. Maggots oozed from her cheeks, crawling in packs around her eyes, nose, lips, neck, and body. Worms spewed, forcing her left eyeball from its socket, squirming in clumps, and falling on Nikki. "We are one," declared Iyana. "Forever. I'm never leaving you."

Thump. Thump. Thump.

Flies and locusts swarmed, thumping against the outside window to enter, feed, and

101

lay new larvae on the decay in the room. Iyana's supernatural grip lessened when one of her arms detached and fell onto the floor. Individual teeth from Iyana's clenched smile chipped, cracked, broke, and shattered like glass on the floor. Her other arm— detaching from her body. Her lower leg— breaking from her knee. Her spine softening into rubber. The rest of her— rotting from the inside out. And as Nikki backed away from Iyana, she screamed at the sight of her own unrecognizable reflection in the mirror.

"Whatever happens to me, happens to you, too, Sis," laughed Iyana's corpse. "Besties for eternity."

Envy
Proverbs 14:30
A sound heart is the life of the flesh: but envy the rottenness of the bones.

CHAPTER 17

"What goes around comes around," explained the tour guide. "And what you put out, you shall receive. Unfortunately for Nikki, the jinx could not be reversed. That's just how magic works. It is true: roots always make it back to the rightful owner. So inevitably, both Nikki and Iyana died together in their own filth at the altar of their undying friendship."

Jamison felt the urge to throw up.

"That's so sick and scary," said Chelsea, shaking her head. "They were frenemies."

The tour guide smiled. "Let's continue now, shall we?" she said, ushering the group further through the mansion.

CHAPTER 18

"The master suite is a spacious room large enough for more than two, considering its size," said the tour guide, opening the door.

"That's a nice-looking family," said Chelsea, studying the framed family portrait of a man, woman, and three children hanging above the bed.

"Why yes," said the guide. "By the looks of it, they are quite a charming family. On the surface, you'd think this family had it all. But what you don't see lies beneath their smiles. The soul tie— the twin flame. Both bonds are nearly impossible to break." Walking closer to the bed, she continued staring at the framed portrait. "You see, Marcus— Marcus had a strong weakness for women, which led to his unfortunate demise. Some people call it fate, others call it karma. Who knows exactly? But this is the story of Marcus."

The tour guide's voice trailed off, vaporizing, leveling into pixelated grains, dissolving and darkening all but the illuminated antique-framed family portrait of their plastic smiles, bringing Marcus into focus.

CHAPTER 19
2025

"Man, have you lost your mind?" asked Devante. "Sharon's gonna kill you when she finds out." Devante tried smacking the ball from Marcus, but his plan was null and void. Marcus made the jumpshot.

"Buckets!" said Marcus. "Bruh, she ain't gon' do nothin'. I got too much *game* for allat."

"Aye, you keep playin' with fire, man, you're bound to get burned. Mark my words," said Devante.

"What's *that* supposed to mean?" Marcus stood with the basketball under his arm, a smug look on his face, and palms up.

Devante sighed, dropping and shaking his head before looking at his friend. "You just don't get it, do you?"

"Dawg, chill the hell out," said Marcus, dribbling the ball between his legs. "I know what I'm doin'."

"Cool. But don't say I didn't warn you," said Devante, smacking the ball from Marcus' hands and making a three-pointer.

"Now, that's real game," laughed Devante. "But in the meantime, I'mma pray for you—cause you need it."

Pssh, Marcus blew a raspberry. "That's the last thing I need."

"Yeah. Whatever, man," said Devante, shaking his head, walking off the court. "I'm out."

Marcus was walnut-brown with a shiny bald head. Average height and partially in shape, he was not built for the professional basketball career he had always dreamed he would have. Presented with no offer, he still imagined his life as a pro-ball player, hopeful until his wife, Sharon, got pregnant in college, changing "everything," according to Marcus.

Despite his pipe dream, his uppity mother-in-law had other plans.

"Nah, see— Marcus triflin' ass needs to get a *real* job. Stop thinkin' 'bout goin' *pro*," she said, her voice carrying through the salon.

"I know that's right," agreed her cosmetologist, slapping hands with her. The salon was packed with walk-ins and clients with standing appointments. They all listened in.

"Ha, ha! Ain't nothin' pro 'bout that man besides that pre-mature balding head of his!" She laughed. "Look, I got *just* the job for Marcus! It's got benefits, insurance, retirement— all a man needs to take care of my Sharon— if he can just get his damn act togetha'!"

"And you think he's gon' give up that baller lifestyle of his?" asked a woman side-eying from the dryer chair.

"Mmm Mmmm!" uttered Sharon's mother, disapprovingly throwing her hands up. Adjusting herself in the hydraulic chair, she bugged her eyes at the woman. "And was I talkin' to *you*?"

The woman under the dryer side-cocked her head, pursed her lips, and rolled her eyes, looking away— getting the picture.

Marcus's mother-in-law's plan worked, securing him a regular nine-to-five with a benefits package for their growing family, officially crushing Marcus's dreams of going pro forever. But his appetite for the stereotypical "baller" lifestyle grew.

While married to Sharon, Marcus had been with so many women he had lost count. He was what you'd call a playa, womanizer, playboy, skirt chaser, philanderer— toxic. He was all those names times ten.

He was an attention-seeking tease. Staring at a woman he was interested in, he'd quickly look away, busying himself with something else, not giving her any more notice. But the look. The stare was the bait. That's what drew the women in, hooking them. He had a lot of fish in the sea, too.

Unintentionally, Marcus breathed in the sinister spirit with each unclean thought, born from an unclean heart, in pursuit of multiple women as a married man. The ominous spirit fed on him, lurking in the shadows of his bedroom, the streets, the hotel rooms, the car— anywhere he committed adultery.

Marcus didn't give a damn if he got caught either. Why would he, when he could just blame his wife for his ill behavior? Any excuse to take the pressure off was his tactic. *Sharon knew what she was getting herself into before she married me,* he often thought, blaming his wife for his problem.

Scheduling a "business trip" was always his way out. This would be his third business trip in the same month. *I need to blow some steam* was his rationale. So, he booked a room at the bed and breakfast per usual.

⁓

"Another conference, Marcus?" Sharon asked after putting the kids down. She knew the truth. He wasn't going to a conference.

Sharon knew Marcus' nature and habits when she first met him— the late-night messages, hiding his website history, flirting with other women— all signs of infidelity. Back then, she ignored the behaviors—young and dumb— thinking she could change him, but nothing changed.

"It's the third time this month," said Sharon, tiredly. "Marcus, when are you going to spend time with me and the kids? We need you here."

But none of that helped. Marcus just stared through Sharon. Grabbing his bag, he walked to the front door without saying a word. Not a "goodbye" or an "I love you." Only silence.

Sharon called Marcus' phone several times. All calls went to voicemail. She left text messages. All texts were unopened. Pacing the floor, fleeting thoughts flew through her mind a mile a minute. She was trying to stay soft, but living with Marcus was hardening her. So, hitting a breaking point, Sharon logged into her husband's online accounts without any trace of suspicion.

Marcus arrived in town to pick up a meal for two and stopped at the store for a few gifts before heading to the bed and breakfast. It was the same building he lived in as a teenager with his grandmother when it was a multiplex. Now, he could discreetly host his new women in the same spot. He smiled, heading to the front door.

"That piece of shit!" Sharon screamed at the computer screen. Reviewing the bank account, she knew what he was up to. Marcus was spending their money to finance his affairs. Sharon was fed up and logged back on online. "This shit ends today."

"Two keys, please," Marcus requested with his best smile on display for the front desk attendant.

"My pleasure," she responded bashfully.

While the front desk attendant checked him in, Marcus checked her out. He looked the girl over, running his eyes over her face, scanning her features, and assessing her assets. She was cute but a little too young. He looked away, unimpressed, but still playing the game.

"Nah, baby. The pleasure's mine," flirted Marcus. Winking with a sly smile before walking away as the girl whispered and giggled with another receptionist. Meanwhile, he wasn't thinking of that girl. He was thinking of

Alyssa. A grown-ass woman who knew how to handle, treat, and take care of a grown-ass man.

He opened the room door and fell on the bed, expecting her to enter the room any minute. Lying across the bed, Marcus thought about what it took to get Alyssa's attention. *It took a lot more effort than a typical chick. But then again— ain't nothin' typical about Alyssa,* he grinned.

Marcus kept tabs on Alyssa. Doing all the things to get her attention— following her on social media, liking her sexy posts, and watching her stories. But she never seemed to respond. And it didn't help that he forgot how to date a woman. He and Sharon had been married for over 12 years, and the last time they dated, the scene was different. But he went the extra mile with Alyssa. So to get her attention, beyond the usual likes and views, he DM'd her and finally got a reply: a splash emoji. That was his window, his door of opportunity, and he, in his mind, slam-dunked on it.

Alyssa entered the room wearing a long black trench coat with 6-inch stilettos. It was summer, so he knew what was up. *She's ready for the taking*, he told himself.

"So, I see you're a family man," said Alyssa, placing her hand on Marcus' chest, close enough for him to breathe her in. "I like that."

"Mmm. Damn, you smell good," he acknowledged, eyeing her arousingly. Alyssa was intoxicating and nothing like his slim, petite, ordinary wife, who constantly complained about everything. The new ones never complained. They were easy to please and happy about shit that didn't really matter. Not much effort was required to make them feel special. *Give 'em just enough to keep 'em satisfied but still hungry for more* is how he handled women.

Alyssa was tall, big boned, and absolutely beautiful. Her hazel eyes were unbelievable, and she had a body that just wouldn't quit, and that satiny, supple caramel skin. He imagined enjoying every bit of Alyssa.

'I saw your pictures online, but I can see this is what you really want." Alyssa began unbuttoning her coat meticulously as Marcus watched, silently seduced.

The dark shadow lurked above the building, floating under the door and into the bedroom.

'Shit!" Marcus yelled out while looking past Alyssa. But she didn't realize his reaction wasn't toward her.

"I know, baby," said Alyssa, giggling. "I'm a lot of woman— your woman, tonight."

What the hell was that? Marcus thought to himself. Squeezing his eyes closed, massaging his eyelids, he tried to wipe away the image he had seen. *Get yourself together,* he coached himself. Then, he remembered. He had seen it before. A few times throughout his life. His first encounter was as a teenager. Marcus remembered staring above the bedcovers as the shadow entered his room, crouching down into the crease of the wall. His bed vibrated and jerked fiercely as the faraway voice spoke in an unknown language, and young Marcus sat unable to move. A doctor said it was "normal sleep paralysis from a bad dream."

Another time, on their wedding day, as he stared into the eyes of his bride, Sharon, at the altar, to the left of her veil, the black shadow emerged in the chapel, rising high, covering the walls and stained glass, and reaching the ceiling, darkening his mind.

"Cold feet" is how he made sense of it over the years, but that explanation still didn't work. Plus, how could he rationalize the other times that left him debilitated by the shadow? He always thought it was just in his head. *Fear of commitment,* he thought to himself, after the wedding, but he couldn't explain the other times. So, he practiced ignoring and forgetting what he saw that no one else could.

When he opened his eyes, the shadow was nowhere in sight. Relieved, Marcus focused on Alyssa. She was undressing herself, slowly removing the coat from her shoulders, letting it drift down her voluptuous body to the floor. She stood in high heels, a black lace bra, and a thong.

Marcus thought about how his wife used to look that good and wear lingerie until she let herself go, becoming too tired after having the kids. Quickly, he erased Sharon from his mind to enjoy his new woman— *sexy, thick Alyssa with them hazel eyes*— taking charge and having his way with her.

"Now, it's my turn," said Alyssa, rotating atop Marcus. Straddling his hips, Alyssa slid down toward his quads, kissing Marcus' body. "Remember, I said, I know what you like?" She ran her wet tongue over his lower abdomen.

"Yeah, baby," he whispered. "I know."

"Good," she said sensually. "Because I have a little surprise for you." Slowly, standing, Alyssa walked seductively to the door. Her oiled and toned body glistened under the dimly lit bedroom lights. Marcus couldn't take his eyes off her. She was a tease, like him.

"And, what's that?" Marcus asked with glimmering eyes and an airy voice. Gently biting his lower lip, staring sheepishly at Alyssa.

"A friend," said Alyssa erotically, opening the door to his wife, who fired one bullet from a semi-automatic gun into the middle of Marcus' forehead and turned the gun on herself. Marcus' naked body lay sprawled on the bed with wide open eyes, bleeding out onto the brain-soaked bedcovers. Meanwhile, Sharon's body lay in a puddle of blood on the floor, allowing the black shadow to exit Sharon's body and leap into Alyssa's, attaching itself like a cloak on her back, and feeding on her like predator and prey.

Lust
Matthew 5:28

But I say unto you, That whosoever looketh on a woman to lust after her hath committed adultery with her already in his heart.

CHAPTER 20

"The same sinister spirit haunting Marcus haunted the women he had relations with," explained the tour guide. "So, be careful with whom you sleep. Spirits travel from body to body, like a disease— or better yet— a parasite bound to its victims until death."

Turning off the lights and closing the door to the master suite, the tour guide escorted the group to a large living room with a fireplace.

"We are standing in the family room, where the most memorable family events often occur. The fireplace, a central part of a home during the antebellum era, had many uses: natural light, heat during cooler weather, and certainly a place for *ghost stories*. Who doesn't like a good ghost story?" The tour guide belted out a high-pitched laugh.

"This woman is nuts," said Frederick inconspicuously.

The guide continued without reading the room or catching the social cues. "Just look at this beautiful fireplace."

"Yeah," said Frederick, snarkily under his breath. "It sure looks like it's seen better days." But the tour guide heard him that time.

"Well, of course– it was quite a jewel in its heyday. Why wouldn't it be? Look at its size. Why, it's big enough to fit a whole body inside." The tour guide burst into laughter again, making the whole room uncomfortable.

The friends stared at each other, puzzled, until Evalina set her eyes on a painting above the mantle of a man with auburn hair and dark brown eyes, standing in a three-piece suit with his left hand halfway in his pocket and the other resting on a corner table. The tour guide noticed.

"That, my dear, is a self-portrait of Monsieur Charles Le Rue de Baptiste," she said, facing the gold-framed painting above the fireplace. "Master Baptiste owned this property, which operated as a model, southern plantation. Indeed– he built it for his wife, Lady Marie, and it certainly was to her liking, as well." Staring at the painting, she continued. "Rumor has it that one night, as Master Baptiste sat in that very chair in this room, he met the hands of death by one of his field slaves, leaving his body unrested in the mansion." Shifting her body away from the portrait to the tourists, she stated, "You may find this story particularly interesting."

CHAPTER 21

"During a time when tobacco and horse breeding were king in Kentucky, the house was built on cursed ground on the banks of the Ohio River in Louisville," said the tour guide.

"The land surrounding the house belonged to the indigenous peoples of the Americas or Native Americans– the Shawnee and Cherokee tribes, particularly. They were forced off their land due to the Indian Removal Act and the Trail of Tears by explorers, colonists, and wealthy businessmen— plantation owners and slaveowners alike.

"Monsieur Baptiste, a prominent member of the aristocracy, managed southern plantation life, following the instructions in the Willie Lynch Letter. He justified slavery with misinterpretations of the Bible and myths about race, which he believed placed African people in their peculiar predicament with the Curse of Ham. His favorite Bible passage was Genesis 9:25, "'And he said, Cursed be Canaan; a servant of servants shall he be unto his brethren.'"

The guide continued. "For the plot of land and acreage he needed for his financial ventures, Monsieur Baptiste requested the killing of the natives who lived on or around the land, as he was to have a house built for and in the liking of his bride, Lady Marie, a refined and graceful woman from an illustrious and wealthy British family that settled in Kentucky.

"When the builder, J.R. Swan, who was also an artist by trade and practicing priest, requested plans for the house, Monsieur Baptiste responded in his native tongue. But Swan was British, like his wife."

"Elle obtient tout ce qu'elle veut," said *Monsieur Baptiste.*

"English. Please, sir," implored Swan.

"Of course," replied *Master Baptiste. "Whatever she wants, she gets."*

The guide continued, "Lady Marie designed and decorated every square foot and inch of the mansion. Five stories overlooking the river. Big windows, shutters, a large wrap-around porch, and three wrap-around balconies with Corinthian columns reminiscent of Rome.

"The mansion was perfect for a French gentleman and a British lady, starting their life together in Kentucky as husband and wife, and soon after, to produce darling children—unlike Lady Marie's spinster sister in Brighton, thank heavens. Monsieur Baptiste was expected to run a lucrative tobacco and horse-breeding and training plantation on the property.

"During the construction of the mansion, Swan followed all directions from Lady Marie, but deviated from the plan, adding his own signature to the ceiling– the Seven Deadly Sins scribed in Latin and painted with gold leaf, modeled after chapels in Europe, requiring a gilding process. He added the encryption reflecting the earliest church's understanding of righteous living, binding the house to the religious monogram upon the ceiling. However, the Baptistes never detected or paid any attention to the true commission of the message."

Holding hands, Lady Marie and Monsieur Baptiste admired their new home at the entrance of the tobacco fields. "It's lovely, dear," said Lady Marie, with tears of joy in her eyes.

"However, the wedding had passed, and still no children. Lady Marie would soon discover that due to unfortunate circumstances, her womb was barren, leaving her childless.

"Over time, although Lady Marie came to terms with her condition, she cried herself to sleep every night and couldn't hide from it. It stared her right in the face as she often caught her husband with Anna, the house slave. It made Lady Marie's insides burn with fury and anger. She'd cry into her pillow, screaming as he chose the slave and not her. And soon, there was talk that the house slave, Anna, who had been pulled away from her husband and children in the field for many months, was with child, further infuriating Lady Marie.

"But, like the proper lady she was, she never spoke of it. To anyone, for that matter.

For the women of her day, departing from their husbands for any reason or speaking of such affairs would have been scandalous. It would have been blasphemy on her part. Slander. So, like many of the women of her racial caste system and social standing, she was committed to silence. But– she still loved him. Oh, how she loved that man.

"Lady Marie was blindly in love with Master Baptiste. So, when it was revealed that Anna had birthed her sixth child, in addition to the five she had with Big John— a field slave, the shade and strength of coffee— but this child bore a striking resemblance to Master Baptiste, it was the *perfect opportunity* for Lady Marie to seize the child for herself."

Lady Marie scowled over Anna lying in the birthing bed, reaching to take the baby from the mother's arms. "The child does not look like a slave," said Lady Marie, holding the baby, and staring toward Master Baptiste, preparing to document his new property in a journal, before suspiciously staring at his wife. "We will raise her as our own," said Lady Marie decisively.

Then, with her eyes to the wall, she spoke in an unnatural, cheerful tone: "The child is mine—yes! I birthed her," she falsely confessed, grinning to her husband for reassurance. He stood, staring at his wife and the mulatto child—his child—pale-faced and speechless. Lady Marie wept, burying her face in her husband's chest while cradling the infant in her arms, speaking between cries. "Darling, look! God has finally blessed us with our own. His countenance is upon our face." Marie held the cream-colored baby close to her milk-free breasts. And when she finished speaking, she shot her eyes at Anna.

Getting a hold of herself, Lady Marie wiped her face, pushed her sweaty hair from her forehead, pulled back her shoulders, and stood upright as a new woman, staring glacially into space and speaking loud enough for Anna, her slave, to hear. "And to nourish the baby and keep her healthy, Anna will serve as the wet nurse, tending to whatever my baby needs."

The tour guide continued, "Idle talk about Lady Marie began to spread across nearby plantations, causing quite an uproar."

"The slaves are beginning to talk amongst themselves about your wife!" explained Sir Richard Thomas. He spoke in a quiet frenzy in the parlor behind closed doors. He, too, was a wealthy plantation owner. "My slaves have gotten lashings for such scandalous talk, but I am sorry, sir. It seems Lady Marie has gone mad! What will you both do with a Negra child? Your reputation, sir, could be ruined."

Having picked up the southern habit of using his own product, Monsieur Baptiste stared into the blue eyes of the round-faced man who spoke of his wife irreverently, allowing the snuff on the right side of his gums to calm his nerves. Studying the man's face, unmoving, he raised his silver cup, spitting the brown tobacco juice into the pool of liquid.

"We will raise her as our own," declared Monsieur Baptiste, speaking diplomatically. "The child is white— and we will not speak of this any longer." Monsieur left the room, leaving his most trusted confidante in the company of his own thoughts.

As the child grew, her race was kept from her. She was fair-skinned with light brown eyes and wavy hair. She was white. And Lady Marie raised her white as her own, despite the child's true birth mother. And

127

everything was perfect with the child, until, at fifteen, tuberculosis buried her in pastel blue ribbons, a matching dress, and lace gloves.

With a shaky voice and teary eyes, the tour guide continued. "Soon afterward, Lady Marie grew gravely ill, contracting cholera. Many had died that year in 1847. With a burning fever, she was bedridden, unable to eat or drink, leading to severe dehydration. And within a week of the doctor's visit, death knocked at her door. Lady Marie turned bluish-gray, falling into a coma. Forgotten in the walls and cracks of this house. A tombstone of a mansion." The tour guide's bottom lip trembled as she paused, captured by the story she was telling.

This is world-class acting, Evalina thought. Not holding back, she clapped as her friends, staring bizarrely at her, gradually joined in applause. The tour guide quickly wiped her eyes with a handkerchief, relaxing her shoulders, and continued.

"Even with his wife on her deathbed, Master Baptiste continued to pursue Anna, Big John's wife. And yet, while she was known to use plants for magic among the other slaves, she did not use her abilities for evil.

"Rather out of fear, Anna hid the rape from her husband. She didn't want any trouble to come to him or their children. Although she was the legal property of Master Baptiste, Big John tried his best to protect his wife and their five children. Thus, when Big John found out this secret, he plotted what would later become one of the most successful slave revolts in the history of the United States of America. He had heard of the Stono Rebellion of 1739 and, most recently, Nat Turner's Rebellion in 1831. Despite the deadly outcomes of both insurrections, Big John was inspired to lead his own successful revolt, willing to risk it all to free his wife, children, and the rest of the enslaved people on the Sacrée Plantation, and he did that night."

CHAPTER 22

"This mansion has seen life, and it has seen death. And that's why you are here," said the tour guide. "Isn't that so? For answers." Smiling, she led the group to the back of the house and unlocked a concealed door to a hidden stairwell. "Follow me."

Reaching the top of the fifth-floor stairs, a black picture in a gold antique frame hung adjacent to a closed door.

"Perhaps what we do not see is the key to unlocking your questions," said the tour guide. "Or, perchance, what we do not see isn't hidden at all." The guide held a metal ring with a single skeleton key around her wrist, unlocking the door and leading the group into the dark, chilly attic. Three people sat cross-legged on the floor, holding hands with their heads bowed. A small photo turned backwards and nailed to the floor sat in the middle of the circle by a burning candle.

"These three friends loved ghost stories and, well, one moonrise, much like tonight, its majestic pull brought them to this house. It was boarded and vacant, but they removed the wooden boards from a window on the porch and entered.

"In this attic, three friends mysteriously disappeared during a ritualistic séance, conjuring the spirit of the dead child whom the Baptistes took from Anna. Legend has it that the child still haunts the corridors of this mansion, luring occupants in search of her true birth mother, while trapped under the diabolical grand master of the spiritual underworld. A magnificent obsession, actually." Turning toward the group, the tour guide continued. "Perhaps you have met the circle of friends?"

"Why would we know them?" asked Frederick.

"You know, sometimes we are blind to what's right in front of us," said the guide. "Sometimes the obvious is hardest to see."

Evalina, Frederick, Chelsea, and Jamison stared perplexed at the tour guide, who smiled, continuing.

"Why, darlings— don't you remember? The power of the séance still lives on today. Just as you have heard the story of the seven visitors who were haunted by the dark spirit in this house, *you* were visitors, as well. We stand here in the mansion where you once lived as a child, Evalina," explained the tour guide. "You are the spirit of the child born to a slave woman named Anna and her master, Monsieur Baptiste. In the afterlife, you roam this house, searching for something real. Something to hold onto. Something to give you answers. As a child often does, you used your imagination and created this fantasy land, this world, exploring this house daily. Enticing people to the only reality you have known on this phantom plantation, Evalina."

Walking to the middle of the circle, the tour guide removed the photo nailed facedown to the floorboards, revealing a picture of a young girl lying in a casket. Standing in the glow of the candlelit circle, Evalina now wore the blue ribbons, dress, and gloves from the daguerreotype photograph of herself. Her friends— Chelsea, Frederick, and Jamison— who had entered the mansion with her, were no longer standing by her side but staring up at her while holding hands, as the three college friends who disappeared in 1991.

Everything Evalina thought she knew about her reality never existed. She was a spiritual fixture attached to the house that the three friends séanced to the circle. The child they heard stories about, who continuously returned to the house, reliving an eternal death.

CHAPTER 23

Years passed, and a historical marker was placed in front of the mansion to honor the triumph of the enslaved Africans who acquired freedom– Big John, his wife Anna, their children, and the other enslaved persons on the Sacrée Plantation, leaving a brief mention of the Baptiste family.

To this day, if you visit the house, you may encounter what many witnesses have experienced: a shadow emerging over the roof shingles, darkening the porch, leaning against the Corinthian column pole, with one leg crossed over the other, holding a glass of 1847-aged Kentucky bourbon as Monsieur Baptiste holding the hand of his wife— the tour guide, Lady Marie with Evalina by her side, awaiting the next visitor.

CHAPTER 24

"No one truly owned the 1847 mansion," narrated Ms. Janelle to the rehab residents. "But make no mistake. This mansion, marked by the sins of racism and slavery, was haunted by an ancient omen dating back to the beginning of time, with the original sin, granting the fallen angel permission to test the free will and choices of God's people.

"Everyone who lived and died in the mansion struggled with something, just like us. Spiritual weakness is inevitable, but the response is the test. Even when guided to the light, each person still chose darkness–possessing them–causing vulnerability and susceptibility to fall into temptation, all traps and tricks of the enemy.

"See, sin *is* the entity: the same evil spirit, but a different monster. So, take heed. While we are not perfect, choice is the most powerful strength we possess."

EPILOGUE

"Hey, Mom! Dad! Someone bought the house!" said the eleven-year-old girl. "Look!" she said, pointing to the "Sold" sign staked into the ground.

No one ever lived there as far as she knew. But she was always fascinated by the house. *It's so beautiful,* she thought, wondering how many rooms it had and what it was like to live there when it was first built.

"We know, sweetie," said her mother, gazing at her smiling husband.

"We bought the house!" exclaimed her father.

"What?! It's ours?" asked the girl in disbelief.

"It's our new home, baby," her mother affirmed, joy written all over her.

Pulling into the newly paved driveway was like a dream. The girl smiled, staring out the window at the house—the sun rays, shifting and twinkling between the golden-green tree branches.

"It looks like a picture," said the girl, marveling at the house in wonderment.

Her mother smiled, turning around and winking at her. "It sure does, sweetie. Now, *we* are in the picture."

And as the girl stared at the mansion from the backseat window, she saw it.

ABOUT THE AUTHOR

Dr. Tytianna Ringstaff, a Michigan native and Kentucky transplant, is a publisher, artist, college professor, and director. With over eight published books, she holds dual bachelor's degrees in English and Pan-African Studies, a master's in Pan African Studies, and a Ph.D. in Curriculum and Instruction. This is her first book of horror fiction. She resides in Kentucky with her handsome husband and their family.

9 781735 251615